The Gravedigger

The Arsenic Lobster

Nahoonkara

Domestic Disturbances

Wait Your Turn and The Stability of Large Systems

The Glob Who Girdled Granville and The Secret Lives of Actors

The Girl on the Swing and At Night in Crumbling Voices

This House That

Kissing the Lobster

half-burnt

The Three-Legged World

Everything Has Become Birds

Last Night I Aged a Hundred Years

Domestic Bestiary

Peter Grandbois

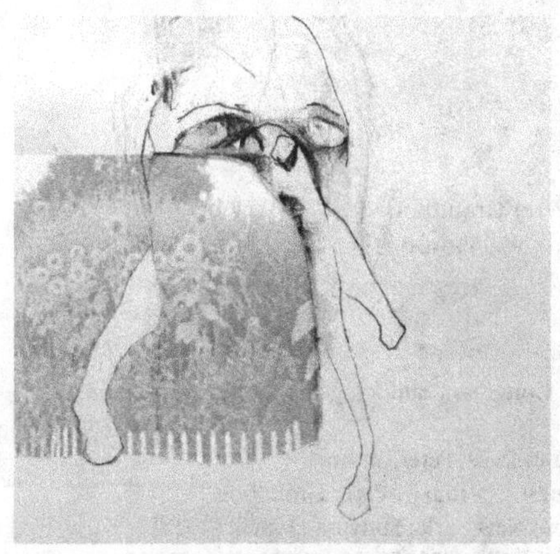

SPUYTEN DUYVIL
New York   Paris

© 2023 Peter Grandbois
ISBN 978-1-959556-06-0

Library of Congress Cataloging-in-Publication Data

Names: Grandbois, Peter, author.
Title: Domestic bestiary / Peter Grandbois.
Description: New York : Spuyten Duyvil, [2023]
Identifiers: LCCN 2022053652 | ISBN 9781959556060 (paperback)
Subjects: LCGFT: Short stories.
Classification: LCC PS3607.R3626 D66 2023 | DDC 813/.6--dc23/eng/20221108
LC record available at https://lccn.loc.gov/2022053652

For Shadow and Drake and Loba
and Makwa and Kyoko
and Sauron and all the rest…

Being alive is inhuman.
—Clarice Lispector

Contents

The Body's First Lesson

My soul would sing of metamorphoses . . .
Ovid

I.

Listen. I'm going to have to speak. There's no oth-er way. A new god was found. There, I said it. But what kind of god I don't know. The present isn't simple like the past. The past is ordered. You can tell a story about the past. So that's where I guess I'll have to start. But how to start. How to recognize what is the start. Something only becomes significant after it happens. Not when. We see after. But even that seeing is artificial. Before we realize we have a story to tell, we've already narrated it over and over in our mind, already made an infinite number of beginnings.

Then there's the problem of form. Form decides which one of the infinite number of stories I reveal. And there's the question of what form I take. I thought I knew what I was, who I was. But I was wrong. I only saw myself as others saw me. No. That's only partly true. I saw myself as I had narrated myself. We are the sum of the stories we tell. And how many of those are true?

"

Before I had a form. And now I don't. It's that simple. That's what I've learned since the event. The story of me is held together only long enough to walk past mirrors but never long enough to look into one, at least not for any length of time. The story of me held together by a name. Barbara. Was that it? I think so. A half-forgotten name. So, how do I tell the story of Barbara?

I had a job, too. I'm almost sure of it. Another story of me. Professor of Theatre, perhaps? Maybe English? I hope it wasn't philosophy, but it could just as easily be that. I remember driving home thinking about theatre. The audacity of attempting to put life on a stage. Or was it a page? Arranging words on a page? Actors on a stage? What's the difference? Once upon a time there was a young girl. That's all we need to know.

II.

Or not so young. Not a girl at all. A woman. Once upon a time there was a woman named Barbara whose husband approached her one morning saying the back-door video camera had caught her standing on the porch staring at the garden for most of the night. He hadn't wanted to bring it up the first time. But there it was on video again the next night and the next. She'd been standing on the back porch from midnight to six am doing nothing but staring at the garden for the last four days. He was starting to get a little freaked out.

What the hell were you doing? he wanted to know. *Have you started smoking pot?* he asked. He'd rifled through her dresser and closet looking for drugs only after he'd heard the audio. He hadn't known there was an audio until just this morning when he stumbled upon the mute button by accident. Even then it was difficult to hear what she was saying.

III.

Once upon a time you were a young girl. Or not so young. Not a girl at all. A woman named Barbara who loved to garden Saturday and Sunday mornings after coffee, weather permitting. You loved the smell of dirt beneath your fingernails so you never wore gloves, and you loved the thistle's sting on your calves so you never wore long pants either. How else were you to know you were alive? You planted parsley and carrots, cabbage and tomatoes. Flowers, too. Daylilies and Poppies. Peonies and Yarrow. You worked the garden because it centered you, or at least you told yourself that. You needed centering. Your husband told you that. After dealing with students who didn't show up for class or didn't turn in assignments or lied about why they didn't show up for class or turn in assignments. After sitting through committee meeting after committee meeting where nothing ever actually got done. After trying to trim the ever-growing list of unanswered emails. You needed centering. And that's when the event happened. That's when you saw it. You were digging holes for your geranium seeds when you dug the thing up. It was so fragile; you were lucky it didn't break. You knew right away what it was. Or at least that's what you told yourself. "A grasshopper," you said under your breath. "It's a dead grasshopper." But it wasn't really that at all, was it? You dusted the dirt off it with your fingers, not sure why you were doing it, only that you wanted to see it more clearly. The dry husk crackled beneath your fingertips. For that's what it was, nothing more than a husk, a shell. The hard exoskeleton that had been discarded.

You took it inside and studied it under the kitchen light. Everything was still there—the legs, the head, the eyes, even the antennae. It was a grasshopper, had all the grasshopper parts, and yet it wasn't. The inside was missing. Or rather, the inside had discarded the outside. The thing that made the grasshopper what it was had discarded its form. How could this happen? I mean you knew that it happened. Happened every minute of every day. But *how* could it happen? And how many times did it happen in a lifetime? You searched grasshopper molting on your smart phone. Five times. The thing that is a grasshopper will leave its body five times throughout its life. What do you do with that information?

IV.

Madness can sometimes lead to discovery. Or, as I'm beginning to understand, discovery can sometimes lead to madness. Every cell in the body is a dream. Every dream creates another body. And how many bodies do we create in a lifetime? The thought staggered me. The thought consumed me. I showered five times that Saturday, each time working harder to scrape the dirt from my fingers, the smell of earth from my skin. Only when I was sure I was clean did I change into my nightgown and lay down to nap. I'd expected to find darkness. I'd yearned for it. The erasure of self that comes with sleep. But when I closed my eyes there was the horned head floating above me. I opened my eyes but the head remained. At first I thought it wanted something from me, and that thought terrified me. I ran out onto our suburban street. There it was again, floating in the sky above my house. I screamed, I was so frightened. Thank God no one was near. I wouldn't have been able to explain myself. I ran back inside and took the husk, burying it in the garden where I'd found it. I threw my nightgown in with the dirty laundry and again went to shower. I closed my eyes beneath the heat of the water, and there floated the head, its empty eye sockets watching me, as if I'd done some forbidden act. After dressing in new clothes, I returned to the kitchen to make myself tea. The husk sat on the counter next to my cell phone. Hadn't I buried it in the garden? I threw it in the kitchen trash and took the bag to the garbage can in the garage. When I returned, the husk sat on the counter next to my cell phone. I scooped it up and scoured the house for a place to hide it. Not the junk drawer—too easy to stumble upon it there. Not at the back of the linen closet—the feeling of it touching my towels, my sheets, the things most intimate to me, made my skin crawl. Under the ring case in my jewelry box. That's it. It could sit on top of my bedroom dresser in plain sight, but not in plain sight. I pulled out the tangled necklaces and bracelets I'd never worn and put them in my sock drawer, making room for the husk to sit delicately on the black velvet at the bottom of the box as if it were its grave. I would not open the box again. Not for anything. After, I made my tea and sat on the sofa. Before long, I'd nodded off. The empty eye sockets peered through me to the other side.

V.

Small holes   Waiting   Bodies hidden in holes
In the middle of   days   Bodies leaning on each
other   Bodies leaning on days   One word
OneJumpingOne   word   OneHolesJumping
        into holes   Or is it out of holes   Out of
breath Nobody'sholes   Nobody's breath
Sky like snow Snowlike static falling   And

through the static we are jumping   Jumping
We are one of them   ONE NO-ONE   It's a
gift   NO-ONE gives this giftDirt   on
our hands   Dirt on our jeans   One word
intowhichcrashes   AN-OTHER Sea
Do you seewhat   you are becomingA partof
whatyouare becoming Jumping throughholes
into that whichyouwere   into that
whichyou will become Jumping   Jumpingright
up   intothe   darksky

VI.

When Barbara woke the next morning she couldn't believe how messy her house was. A calm accumulation of dust lay upon the end tables and lamps, mantle and armoire, the chairs and coffee tables—everything. She grabbed her lemon Pledge and a clean rag from the laundry room and set to work. She mopped the hardwood floors of the family room, wiping down every surface until it shined, then moved to the living room and did the same. Then on to the dining room. But when she returned to the family room to sit, the dust seemed piled higher than ever. As if she hadn't done a thing. She sprayed the entire contents of the Pledge can onto the two end tables and the fireplace mantle, thinking if only she could get this room clean, the rest could wait. She scrubbed and scrubbed, and it appeared to be working. The end tables glistened, the mantle shined. She went to the kitchen for water, but when she returned, the family room looked as if she'd never cleaned at all, as if years had passed in the time it took her to walk to the kitchen and back. Worse still, the sickly-sweet smell of decay filled the room. Must be the ferns on each side of the fireplace, she thought. The ferns had collapsed, their leaves browned and decayed, fungi growing from the detritus covered soil in the pots.

She forgot why she'd entered the room. Further, the more she stood there, the more she became confused. It wasn't that she'd stepped into nothing but rather that she'd stepped outside it. Outside the room. Outside the nothing. Outside herself. She ran her finger through the dust on the end table and studied the trail she made as if somehow she was creating a language that would tell her what was going on. She traced more trails in the dust until she was surprised to see the outline of a grasshopper. She turned back to the room but it no longer seemed like a room. Or rather, she couldn't tell where the room began and where it ended. Its contour had shifted. The shades that distinguished the shadows of corners had blurred. At first it seemed like one long hallway without end. But then just as quickly changed until she wasn't sure the room had walls at all.

VII.

You try to leave the room but trip on the area rug. That's when you feel the floor moving, the ground alive beneath your touch, rippling in waves. Is it an earthquake? You don't see anything else shaking. The lamps remain perfectly still. The pictures of long dead relatives that line the shelves beside the fireplace remain standing. The clock on the wall remains on the wall. Your hands leave palm-sized prints in the dust on the floor when you move to stand. You walk toward the clock, its ticking the only sound in your ears. Its ticking filling your body. Until you have no body. Until the sound is your body. And you are riding on that sound. You stand before the clock. At first it looks as if the second hand isn't moving. But then it does move, like an antenna, twitching, it moves a little more with each ticking of the clock. The movement irritates you. In fact, it enrages you. You smash the clock with your fist. And still the second hand keeps twitching. You extend your pointer finger, try to fix that second hand in place, but you can't seem to pin it down. Whenever you think you have it, it keeps moving as if your finger weren't there. That's when you see the two other hands—the minute and the hour—pointing like horns atop an insectoid head at eleven and one.

VIII.

I don't know how old I am. Only that I'm a child again. I'm lying in bed with the covers pulled to my chin. I've tucked the blankets into my side as well so there can be no empty space. Empty space is the enemy. A hand can fit into empty space. A hand with a claw. A hand that wants to reach out and grab me and pull me into the darkness. In this way, I've pinned myself to the bed. I've fixed myself into the exact center of the bed. Only the center will do. If I'm too far to the left or the right, the hand can reach up from under the bed and grab me and again pull me into the darkness. The closet door must remain open. Not all the way open, just halfway. Open exactly halfway. Enough to see in but not enough for the monster that lives there to get out. I lie there in my prison bed, fixed in place, not moving. To move would be to risk opening up a pocket of emptiness. And so my legs and feet touch each other. My hands lie crossed over my chest, and I wait for the night to take me. The only sound the ticking of the glow-in-the-dark clock on the wall. The minute hand on the one. The hour hand on the eleven. In the dream it is dark. I'm walking home, but home is miles and miles away. And now it's dark. And there are no lights anywhere. No cars on the road. And I am afraid. I should not be walking alone. But I am alone. And then I am jumping. Jumping. Right up into the dark sky.

IX.

Once upon a time, Barbara was an old woman. She loved it when her grandkids came to visit, though her husband, let's call him Matthew, wasn't particularly thrilled. He'd learned to love the solitude and quiet of an empty house after the kids had grown. But Barbara had never learned to embrace the emptiness the way her husband had. She'd rather it were filled. And so she moved down the street from her grandkids and invited them over often. In fact, she made cookies nearly every day to entice them to stop at her house on their walk home from school. The gingerbread smell wafted down the street like a song leading them home. She sat at the kitchen table with her two grandkids chatting away all afternoon until their mother, Barbara's daughter, called. "I'm so sorry," Barbara would say to her daughter on the phone when her daughter complained that the kids had homework to do and piano lessons to attend. "I lost all track of time," she would add, as if that explained everything.

She tried to fall the same way into her conversations with Matthew. But it rarely worked that way. He'd warn her to be careful. He'd tell her she was putting too much of herself into those grandkids. He'd say that she needed to find something for herself, or at the very least with him. He'd talk on and on until something would shudder loose inside her and she'd leap from the table with this excuse or that, usually to step out into her garden and wait for the next day when the grandchildren would be lured once again to her home by the smell of cookies in the oven.

X.

Deadalive woman. You start each day that first week by opening your jewelry box, removing the husk from beneath the ring case and holding it for a minute before returning it to its home. You'd swear the antennae quiver, the compound eyes unable to move yet taking in myriad images of you. How many yous exist in those eyes? Are some dead and some alive? And that's when you notice there are three more eyes. Three small eyes beneath and between the two large ones. Five eyes to take in all of you. Five eyes to fix you. Five eyes to pin you until you feel nothing. Nothing at all.

Then it spits on you. It sounds crazy. Maybe it is crazy. But you swear it spit on your face with its brown juice. What other explanation do you have for the anger that followed? Why else would you have smashed the carcass on your dresser, then taken the jewelry box and hit the dried-out husk over and over again, grinding it into the cherry wood until only dust remained and the jewelry box splintered.

That's when everything changed deadalive woman because that's when you couldn't stop seeing the face, that's when it embedded itself in your mind and that's when you started night-walking, and your husband caught you on camera. It's also when you realized the anger inside you, felt its force. You were emerging into something greater, something stronger. You were sure of it.

XI.

I don't want what I saw. Silence. Emptiness. The slow demolition of my life. I moan out loud. So loud I startle the dog who rises from his nap and looks at me cock-eyed. I moan again. An awful moan like pus rising through skin. The dog growls at me. I close my eyes and wait for the sound to pass, wait until it's only the potential for sound that scorches my throat. I feel my body churning as if through mud. I want to follow it, but don't dare. I don't want this life. This truth. This mad canticle. And still my body churns. The mud seethes and shifts. I raise my hands above my head like two deer emerging from the forest at twilight. But it's already too late. I'm breaking loose from myself. I can feel it. I cross to the kitchen, grab my keys and get in the car.

On the way to work I feel more like myself. Or rather like the old me. The one I want to remain. Is that it? I'm afraid, I think. Afraid of what? Changing? Changing into what? This thing that is opening in me. This

13

thing like a thousand moths flying through me. But going where? Is that what scares me? That I don't know where? Or that I know all too well where this leads? It's hot, and I open the driver-side window. But the breeze doesn't help.

I try to tell myself the story of what is happening, but as soon as I start it gets jumbled. Once upon a time, there was a middle-aged professor who . . . When I began all this, I thought it would be easy to tell the story. But now. Now it's actually happening. As if telling and being are the same. And that's when a grasshopper flies through the window and lands on my chest.

I jump in my seat and clench the wheel tight, looking for a place to pull over. Calm down, I tell myself. It's okay. But then it starts crawling up my chest, and I feel its antennae tickling my neck, and it's all I can do to keep myself from running the car off the road. "Scream," I tell myself. "Scream!" but nothing comes out. If I screamed I would unleash the moths flying in my chest. If I screamed I would exit one world and enter another. And though I have no idea what that world would be, I know I'm not yet ready for it. The grasshopper continues its inexorable march up my neck and onto my chin. I shake my head violently trying to dislodge it. I swerve out of my lane then back between the lines. I need to get to the side of the road before I hurt someone. Its antennae now tickling about my mouth,

as if searching for a way in. I look down at the grasshopper. I stare deep into its five eyes, and my world
goes black.

I wake on the side of the road, not sure how I got
there. The grasshopper is gone. My first thought is that
I am naked. I run my hands over my body, feel the den-
im of my jeans, the cotton of my blouse. No, I'm fully
clothed. The road stretches out before me. Silence whis-
pers in my ear, entirely incomprehensible.

XII.

Once upon a time, there was a woman named Barbara who wrote a letter to herself while lying in bed:

> Dear Barbara,
>
> My love, do you see where you are going? Do
> you see how far into your own fear you are trav-
> eling? Do you see how if you continue down this
> path you will lose everything? Why doesn't that
> seem to matter to you? Have you noticed how all
> you are writing is questions? Do you have any
> answers? You only have what you are. So what
> happens when that you that you "have" chang-
> es? Do you still have it? And what are you now?
> What are you now that you are changing? Can
> you exist at all in the middle of such churning
> violence? What happened to you yesterday in the

car? Does it matter if you understand? And what about what you want? Does that matter? Can you translate what you want onto this page? If you could, would it matter? Would it matter that Barbara was a woman who had a fine life, a wonderful life? She had a husband that loved her, who adored her? She had a profession and colleagues that respected her? Would that matter? Would it change anything? What questions frighten you the most, Barbara? Is the world human? Are we human? Am I human?

Sincerely,

B

Of course her husband found the letter. She'd left it on her pillow. And of course he wanted to talk with her about it. The letter frightened him as much as it frightened her. He made a vegetarian risotto because chopping the vegetables calmed him, poured himself a glass of pinot noir, then sat at the kitchen table petting the dog, waiting for her to return from work.

"How was your day?" he asked, as she poured her own glass.

"Long," she replied, then tasted the wine. "Ooh, this is nice. Where'd you find it?" she remained behind the counter, unsure why she wasn't willing to cross to him.

"It's a new one they started carrying." He pulled the

letter from his pocket, smoothed it out on the table. "What's this about?" he asked.

She had to cross to him. She knew she needed to cross to him. And yet, she didn't. "What?"

"This letter," he said. "I found it on your pillow." He held it up for her to see. "Did you write this?"

A good question. A question she knew she couldn't answer. Had she written it? Yes, her fingers had held the pen. But what did that mean? "I don't know," she replied.

He stood, waved the letter in her face. "What the hell is that supposed to mean?" She didn't answer. He took another sip of wine, almost spilled it. Then he read from the letter: *What happened to you yesterday in the car?* "Yes. Barbara. What happened? You don't tell me anything it seems anymore. I feel like I hardly know you." He put the letter on the counter, pushed it toward her. "What happened yesterday in the car?"

She didn't know how to respond. What could she possibly say? A grasshopper jumped through my window, and I entered a fugue state. How could she say that? She couldn't even face him. She forced herself to look at him. "I don't know," was all she could say.

He shook his head in disbelief. "What kind of answer is that?" He took another gulp of wine, then set the glass on the counter. "Why are you keeping secrets?" He put a hand on each of her shoulders. "Look at me," he said. "I care about you. I want to help. What is going on?"

She pulled away. Not because she didn't desire his touch, didn't need his touch, but because his touch made her aware of her own inhumanness.

"Are you having an affair?" he asked, the fear of the unspoken limning his mouth. "I don't feel like I know you anymore. You're not letting me in."

"No," she said. At least she could say that unequivocally. At least she was certain of that. Still, she couldn't look him in the eyes.

"What then?" he asked, reaching for her once again. "What is going on? I'm your husband. I deserve to know."

So this is how it begins, she thought. The shift. The change. The end of who she was. How could she remain herself if she couldn't even explain to the person closest to her what was happening? "Something's calling to me," she managed to say.

"What?" her husband replied. "What are you saying? What's calling to you?" He shook her. Not violently, but as if trying to wake her. "Please make sense."

And suddenly she knew what frightened her. She knew why her life had been a lie. Why life was a lie. Why she was turning toward some other madness or reality, she still wasn't sure which. That need to make sense. To make order. The need that drove her marriage, her job, everything. That need was a lie, a lie to cover up the horror she was moving toward.

"I can't," was all she said.

"Okay." He sat back at the kitchen table. "I love you. You know that." He traced patterns on the tablecloth with his fingers for a long moment. "I love you," he said again. "I can wait."

She turned from him, as if he were the answer she feared.

XIII.

It's a Saturday in late summer, and you emerge into your garden in the early morning light to find the Amaryllis starting to yellow. Everything is alive, you think. And everything dies. Not particularly profound, but it leads to the thought that frightens you more—everything alive changes. And when it changes, the thing it was dies. Life is a series of goodbyes.

You trim one leaf then another. "You are the same as that flower," you whisper, so faint you're not sure you said it. Then you cut away the head of that flower. It's the only way. You cut off another. And another. Do you have the courage to follow it? Was that you again, Barbara? The only answer is to take the pots into a dark corner of the unfinished basement where they can lie dormant. You water them, but only half as much as normal. Next week, you'll water half that. The following week, half again, until the Amaryllis go to sleep. Sleep. Another word we use to order, to make sense of things. How convenient a word is sleep. It allows us to talk of death, of violent change as if all we were doing was lying down for a long winter's nap.

You are the same as that flower, you say again as you emerge from the darkness of the basement. You repeat it on each stair until you're almost sure you believe it.

XIV.

I got scared because I don't know what I'm emerging into. I'm not scared any more. But how to tell the story without hiding? We are always hiding. The habit is too strong. And how to tell a story that includes the body since that is all and everything. How to tell a story that takes into account the inside, the entrails, the wetness and gore, the blood and mucus, piss and shit. How to tell a story of the body when words cannot translate. I say "blood" and you might see something red, you might even remember its metallic taste in your mouth the time you sliced your finger while cutting the onions. But you won't know the force of its push and pull. You can't locate the troubling beauty of its life pulse in a word. And how to tell a story that doesn't sound like a cry for help when living itself is one continual cry. When every word we utter demands a story . . . *and then . . . and then . . . and then . . .* and as soon as we order time we become beggars for another who will listen to our story.

I have glimpsed where I'm going. I've looked into the entrance, and I am scared. But what troubles me most is how to tell a story that is the now, the nothing that I have seen, when the very act of telling turns the now into the ordered past. How to tell a story and remain in the now when the now means to feel and to feel means to put away words. I must jump. There is no other way. Jump and Jump and Jump. And with each haunted jump abandon my human salvation. Words cannot hold me.

XV.

You don't know how old you are, only that you're a child again. You stand in the gully before the entrance of the sewer pipe, watching the water trickle out through the mud. You gauge whether you could fit inside the pipe. Could you stand up or would you be on your hands and knees? There's only one way to find out. You take off your shoes and leave them just outside the entrance. It turns out you only have to bend your head slightly. You're surprised by the feel of the wet mud on your feet, between your toes. The squish and suck with each step. You're also surprised by how many other things exist in the mud. Hard things. Sharp things. Soft things. Furry things you step on. The light lasts for maybe one hundred feet. Probably less. And when you finally get the courage to dig in the mud and see what you've stepped on, it's too dark to see whatever it is you've pulled from the mud.

You keep walking until the darkness is so thick you can taste it. You keep walking until the air suffocates, until the air is so thick it's like inhaling a blanket that has been laid over your head. And then you stop. It's not that you're afraid to go on, though that is also it. Rather, it's a need you feel in your body. A need to take in the darkness, the nothing. To breathe it into you. To let it inhabit you. Become you. You stay like that until you can no longer tell if you're breathing. And you do not move. To move is to do. To do is to exist outside the body.

You remember thinking there are no stars and being surprised by the thought. The only other times in your life you encountered darkness, it was a darkness lit by stars. There's no pain here either. No happiness. No feeling at all. No shades of darkness. Just the darkness itself. You remember the relief of not having to distinguish between shades.

And then you realize your hands have vanished. Your legs have vanished. Your feet that only moments ago were so acutely aware of every contour within the mud are now gone. Your torso is gone. Your face. For the first time since you stopped moving in the tunnel you begin to worry. What if your face is gone, too? You cannot bring your hand to touch your face because you have no hands. A sort of shivering happiness moves through you, a happiness tinged with terror. You've fought all your life against this feeling. You will fight it for the rest of your life. And yet here it is. Deep in this sewer pipe. You let the darkness touch you. You let it move through you. You raise your hand that is not a hand to the sky above and where you thought you'd find the cement ceiling of the sewer pipe, you find nothing. Nothing at all.

You wonder why you have forgotten this memory until now. What mystery was tied to its dormancy?

XVI.

Once upon a time Barbara was dead and gone. Listen to this history of mothers and daughters. Her daughters made cookies each afternoon for their granddaughters, so that the granddaughters caught the scent as soon as they exited the school bus. Those granddaughters sat giggling as they ate their cookies and drank their milk and thought nothing of their great-grandmother, Barbara. She did not exist for them except as a stranger's face in one portrait on top of the bookcase in their parents' living room. Those granddaughters sit inside their cage getting more plump with each cookie, growing swollen with a fear they don't understand because they have not yet named it. And Barbara's daughters say to the granddaughters: "Keep eating, my children. Keep eating, for you are not yet human."

And Barbara's house is long gone, her garden long rotted. In place of both, a bigger, grander house for another Barbara, or perhaps an Alice or Kate. Any residue of her life has been razed. A white sun shining down over all. Did she invent her entire life? Did she make it all up? Did she make up what happened in the garden in hope of being, of existing for that one brief moment?

XVII.

It was a Saturday, and I couldn't stand to be in the house another minute. I took the dog for a walk in the bioreserve. It hadn't rained for quite some time and the dry September ground kicked up dust. With each step, I felt as if I were abandoning another part of myself. Like breadcrumbs. Only I wasn't sure I wanted to find the way back. Occasionally, when the dog stopped to smell something or to pee, I would call out into the woods. *Barbara? Barbara?* But if she answered, I couldn't hear it.

I let the dog lead me off the path and into a meadow. *Please don't abandon me*, I said. To the trees? To the dog? I don't know. Had I already abandoned myself? Left it in the woods? I stood naked in the middle of the meadow with the dog sniffing through the clothes scattered around me. Nothing else matters, I thought.

Nothing else matters but this. This moment. A grasshopper hopped onto my forearm. I could feel the sticky fluid oozing from the hairs on its feet. The pinch of the two spiked hooks that held those feet fixed to my skin. Its two antennae like horns frightened me at first as they tickled my skin. But then I remembered I'd already entered this place and that fear was nothing here. Its five eyes watched me, and I watched it, neither of us moving. Was this the face of God? I wondered. But as soon as I said it, I knew that was another lie. Another story. And then a second grasshopper jumped on me. And a third.

My first instinct was to run, to abandon this new self that was starting to form. But I did not run. I was past running. Though clearly not past all fear. Maybe we never completely lose that. If we did, what excuse would we have? More and more grasshoppers landed on me. On my arms, my legs. On my face and in my hair. I let go the dog's leash, and she wandered off after other smells. And still the grasshoppers came. I was covered by them. Hundreds. Maybe thousands. I don't know. I heard something like my dog barking in the distance. And then silence.

I really don't know how to go on with the story. I don't know what more words can say. But I've pulled you through this far. I've given you my words, and you've innocently taken them inside you. You've come this far with me. And I won't abandon you in the woods. Though I can't promise I can save you from this terror. Maybe you don't want me to. Maybe you're like me after all. The thought makes me cry. I don't know if it's from happiness or sadness. Only that as I stand in the meadow clothed in grasshoppers I taste the salt of tears on my lips. I taste the fear of being lost. And I enjoy it.

XVIII.

Once upon a time a woman named Barbara clothed herself in grasshoppers and nothing would be the same after that.

The next morning she lay trembling on the bed long after her husband left for work, staring at the sky through the window across from her. Where before there had been shades of grey, contours to the clouds, now there was nothing. A vast expanse of grey that at one time had felt oppressive to her. Now it was as though she could see through the grey to the most vulnerable of realities. A reality more secretive than air. A reality she could inhale. Was it the truth? She didn't know. She feared she could only handle part of that truth, anyway. A very small part. She tried to speak the truth but words were enormous. Bigger than the clouds, and they couldn't escape her tiny body. Now it was as if she were suffocating from the inside. Choking on something that had always been inside her.

She rose from the bed and opened the window to the chill autumn air. And that's when she saw it. A giant grasshopper head outlined in the sky, the antennae like horns. The head she thought she had banished when she smashed the dried-out husk. The large, dark eyes bored into her. She forced herself to stare into those eyes, not knowing what to expect. Or did she? Did she expect to see every moment of her life up to this point? Did she expect to see the future? Did she expect an answer to the terrible churning inside her, to the questions that would not stop? She saw the moist cave of night. She saw the dark depths of the ocean. And she saw that she must plunge into that cave, those depths in order to breathe.

Then the white sun broke through the clouds and slowly burnt away the grasshopper head, and she knew what love was. That burning light. That scorching flame that both ended the terror and any possibility of escaping the terror, of plunging into those depths. *I understand!* she thought. *I understand! And the only way through is a secret jumping into the dark sky.* Then she fainted naked on the floor.

XIX.

We know very well   wherewe have to go   We
know   how the world shinesbeneathnight's   waters
and   how the   clockticksfromtimetotime

like thousands   of mouthsopening   and closing
We know   howswiftlyeverythingblursuntilyou
are a ghostinside   a ghostinside   a ghost We
must wash ourselves   free   of words   We
must wash ourselvesfreeof   the shameof light
We must open   to   the longdreamTrace   the
face of God   in the sky   until   we are not nearly   human not   nearlyhuman   not nearly above
or below   pain   Until we can   remember.
Will you   rememberwithme?   Will   you
listenwithme?   Listen   Don't be   afraid

XX.

Matthew sat down the next morning before work
and played back the porch video taken from the night
before. His hand trembled as he held his coffee. His face
moist with sweat as he watched the grainy black and
white.

He saw his wife standing naked on the porch facing
the garden, her back to the camera, her white cotton
nightgown lying beside her feet. The quality was poor.
It was difficult to see anything in the darkness beyond
her body. But he could have sworn there were figures
jumping up and down in that darkness. Hundreds of
horned figures jumping at the edge of the light. They
looked like grasshoppers though much larger than
normal grasshoppers. He tried to adjust the light con-

trast on the monitor but it only made things worse. He couldn't make out shades, contours beyond the light. Nothing was distinct. The more he looked, he wasn't sure of what he saw. Maybe it was just the grainy vibrations of a bad signal, distortions from a poor cable connection.

And then his wife started bobbing. Slowly at first. Just a slight bend in the knees. Almost as if she were dancing. Bobbing up and down in time with the grainy black and white distortions at the edge of the darkness. Her first jump startled him. It seemed higher than a normal jump. She jumped again. So high, as if she were jumping into the dark sky. She jumped in place again and again. He thought he heard something. Her voice distorted almost as much as the figures at the edge of the light. He played it back. Yes, it was her voice. It had to be. "One. I am one," she said. And there was something else. Something she said so softly he had to play it back several times. "How luxurious the silence." He was almost sure that was it. And then she jumped off the screen. He sat down at the kitchen table, sipped his coffee, and stared out the window into the blank sky.

Everything Falls Silent

The cricket's chirp casts shadows doubling us against the darkness, calling to us through unused hours, transferring its nothingness to us, and the more we search for the source of that nothingness, the more it penetrates every pore, every thought, until we become the nothingness, and that's why we search so hard, that's why we never give up looking once we hear it—we scour the corners, beneath the couch, the end table, the arm chairs, behind the vents, even beneath the pile of wood beside the fireplace—we rummage through memory that spills over to the unspoken, the future with its many eyes, the photographs where we keep the dead, and the kingdom of pencils where we keep our pain, but the ghosts we follow don't necessarily follow us, they keep no appointments as they charm the lid off night, break the back of day, and no matter what we do they won't come out, but lie awake in the dark, in the dusty corners, calling us, they won't come out no matter what we do, not for bits of food left on the floor, not for stomping in circles on the hardwood, not for love—they're still there, breathe them in, there's no mistaking their aroma, the smell of time, of lost appointments and hands drifted apart, and that which passes from their body to ours, my body to yours, wants us to live, begs us to inhabit those legs and antennae, that head, but how can we trust it, as if it were so easy to leave this body, to listen to this song that reminds us of our fear of leaving and of life, of accidentally stepping off the edge of the world, and still we search, for what else can we do, and if we found it, what then, would we smash it in the closet door, watch as the guts oozed out, or stomp it with our boots and later scrape the bits off with a butter knife, would we box it and take it far away where we could no longer hear its song, or would we simply walk past, like the mouse that is no longer afraid, and if we did that would we still be thankful for its mystery, for the inversion of words and worlds that makes music of our tiny but inescapable loneliness?

How Ordinary the Revelation

I left my beak hanging on the tree, but my voice continues in my head. There's no silence in this house. No forgetting. No beginning of forgetting. Humans walk by with their widening language, their twitching wings. They don't understand we must be quiet to hear the universe. *This is why we must suffer,* it says, as I hop and flutter. *This is why the sky is clear and empty. Caw. Caw. Caw.* Humans can't see the words that gather here, and so visit some place else. Words like a clattering gate I can't fly through. Were I less naked to myself I might look back to days sewn tight with illusion. Days with eyes washed clean of words and the memories they bring. Like the day my brother stood beneath my tree, calling to me, his face a cacophony of mistakes. I pecked and poked at his weakness, scoffing at his caws for help. *Why can't you be more like me?* I said. *Why can't you do anything right?* He went far away, and at first I didn't care. Later, my sorrow flew on and on. Night after night, I dreamed him back into existence, and in that way my sad brother returned to me. We'd paint the town together, picking up a shiny beer can here, a glistening bauble there. In my dreams I tell him *I understand,* but then he looks at me like a drunk vagabond, and the words fall back to earth, as false as all those pecks and pokes. And so I left my beak hanging on the tree, and still my voice continues in my head.

The ornithology professor told the student to look through the telescope set at the base of the pine grove and report back every detail about the bird. The student closed one eye, peered into the long tube, and jumped back immediately. "A golden eye," he said. "A giant, golden eye." The professor laughed. "You mean a Great Horned Owl or Bubo Virginianus," he said. "It's one of the most common owls in North America, and one of the fiercest predators. It can hunt and kill prey larger than its two-foot size, though commonly stalks its natural enemy, the crow." The professor smiled then gestured the student to take another look.

The student approached, slower this time, scanning the pine forest before looking through the scope. There it was again! The eye filling the entire view. The angry black pupil at the center the only thing breaking the spell of golden fire. He fought the urge to pull away, to escape the all-consuming gaze. "Make careful note of what you see," the professor said. "So you can record it in your field book later. Note the plumage. The white patch at the throat. The reddish-brown facial disc. The tufted feathers commonly called horns but known in the scientific world as plumicorns." The student stepped back, shaking his head as if to escape the vision. "All I see is an eye."

The student turned to the professor, a question on his tongue, but was startled by his beak-like nose. Had his nose always been that way? And then there were the professor's eyes like tiny black beads. He hadn't noticed that before either. Something akin to hunger stirred inside him. "Why doesn't it move?" he asked. "The eye, I mean." The professor gestured to the student's unopened textbook, lying on a rock by his backpack. "Owls don't have eyeballs like humans do," the professor pontificated. "Their eyes are tubes. Fixed in place. That's why they turn their heads around to see." The professor cocked his head sideways as if to better see further up the pine-covered hillside. "Take one more look. See if you can note their zygodactyl claws, two forward facing, two rear. They use them to sever the spines of their prey before swallowing them whole." The student slowly stepped toward the telescope, grabbed the tripod for support, closed one eye and brought the other to the lens. There it was. That golden eye larger than the sun. "Do you see?" the professor's voice cawed behind him. "Yes," he replied.

"Do you really see what I'm talking about?" the professor cawed louder or perhaps nearer this time. "I see everything," the student replied, "Everything there is to see." The professor's hand rested on the student's shoulder, then nudged him to step away. "I don't think you're getting the whole picture," the professor said.

"Let me show you." But the student didn't budge. The eye wouldn't let go. In the distance, the student heard a faint, "Who." The sound repeated, and as it repeated, it seemed no longer to be coming from far away but rather from inside him. "Who," "Who," "Who." The sound filled the student's body in the same way the eye filled his head. The eye grew larger and larger until the student became the eye.

"No," the professor cawed, the sound competing with the "Who" in the student's ear. "You're not seeing what I need you to see." The professor tried to pull the student from the telescope, but the student didn't move. "We need to get going," the professor continued. "Birds wait for no man!"

The student faced forward, claws clenched around the tripod, only the head turning to look behind. There the professor stood, hopping and squawking on and on about something, black feathers polluting the golden fire that burned about the world.

What if When We Leave the Room
There is No Room?

I've given up on sleeping. I listen to the scratching in the walls. It begins after midnight and doesn't stop until I fall asleep. If I fall asleep.

I live in a basement apartment. There hasn't been much work for anyone. Not anymore. So I've been stuck in this place with an air vent above my bed. The worst scratching comes from that vent on the nights I wake from dreaming of bones lifting out of my skin. Whatever's on the other side—a mouse, a rat, a squirrel is desperately trying to scratch a hole to somewhere else.

I have no explanation for the fact that it took me weeks to open the air vent to look inside. I'm not scared of mice, though I might scream if I saw a rat. One time, I did grab a screwdriver from the junk drawer and set it on my bedside table, but I never actually opened the vent. I have no excuse. No logical reason. Except maybe the scratching is what kept me here, in the apartment, or rather the listening to the scratching. Which is maybe why I finally opened the vent the night the scratching stopped. 1:42am.

The silence was worse than the scratching. The silence opened like a great eye that kept watching me. A giant eye made of silence. It was unbearable. I opened the vent and peered inside but couldn't see a thing. I grabbed my cell from the bedside table and used the flashlight app.

There it was—a tiny mouse caught in a glue trap. I hadn't placed the trap there. I don't believe in killing things. The previous owner must have done it. The mouse looked as if it had given up. It wasn't squeaking or anything, just twitching its nose a little with each breath, as if that's all the energy it had left, as if it no longer cared. But that's only half the story. You see, behind the mouse there was a snake with its mouth open as if it was just about to gobble up the mouse. I have to admit when I saw the snake, my heart jumped, and I pulled back from the vent. I'd thought it was going to lunge at me. The snake was black so it was difficult to tell how big it was, but I could see it was bigger than you'd think could fit in a vent. A rat snake, probably. Once I calmed down, I realized how foolish I'd been. The snake was as stuck as the mouse. And as alive, too. I could see it flicking its tongue just out of reach of the mouse, as if it could almost taste it. I screwed the vent lid back on, leaving the mouse and the snake as they were.

I didn't even try to sleep after that. I just sat there in bed listening to nothing, or rather listening to my own thoughts whirling around in my head over and over, going nowhere, like the scratching. I wondered how long they'd been there like that, the mouse and the snake. I wondered who became stuck first. It seemed obvious that the mouse would have been stuck first and then the snake got stuck trying to eat the mouse. But then I wondered if it was possible the snake had gotten stuck first and the mouse just happened to pass by. Admittedly, this made less sense, but the thought still tortured me. The uncertainty of it. Because each scenario meant something completely different if you thought about it long enough, and I thought about it all the time. I had nothing else to do. Nothing else to occupy my life the way I once had a job, a family to distract me from such things.

If the less likely scenario were true, and the snake became stuck first, that would have meant that the mouse knowingly wandered in front of the snake, which introduced the question of why. A question to which I had no answer, or at least no answer that satisfied. Was the mouse taunting the snake? Was the mouse unaware of the snake's predicament and therefore suicidal? A third possibility occurred to me. Was the mouse blind? Literal blindness was unlikely, but still possible. But there was also the possibility of metaphoric blindness, i.e. the mouse was somehow unaware the snake posed a threat. There were certainly examples of this kind of thing in nature, animals, particularly the young of different species, species who normally were deadly enemies, but somehow in this case played together, or even developed some kind of symbiotic relationship. It was possible. I don't know how long I spent considering the less likely scenario, only that days had passed before I realized what I was doing, how I'd created my own metaphoric blindness. I'd allowed myself to focus on that less likely scenario only to escape the horrible ramifications of the much more likely scenario—that the mouse had become stuck first and the snake trapped only when it tried to catch the mouse.

There were two points of view, two possibilities, to consider in this scenario. The first possibility, and the one I originally thought the more horrific, was to see the whole thing from the point of view of the snake, the snake who sat there with its meal inches from its mouth, a meal that could easily satisfy its growing hunger, and yet, it would never eat that meal, could never eat it no matter how much it wanted to. The thought of that unsatisfied desire consumed me until the second more horrific point of view popped into my head, the scenario that has haunted me ever since. I wish I understood the workings of the human mind. I wish I understood why we, each of us, will eventually land on the one thought that will drive us mad. Why the mind seems determined to find that thought regardless of the consequences. It happens sooner or later to everyone. For me, the moment came when I considered the point of view of the mouse who became stuck first and was unable to turn around, the mouse who had no idea the snake was behind it, mouth open, poised to strike.

I couldn't rid myself of the image. Whatever I did, whether it was eating, reading, or watching TV, eventually, I'd see that open mouth in my mind's eye, feel it behind me. But when I'd turn around, there was nothing there. Sleep, the few times I was able to sleep, didn't help. I dreamed of a mouth waiting to swallow me up. And holes everywhere, holes that would suddenly appear as I was walking to the fridge or walking to the TV. It was almost as if I became the mouse, or rather, as if I became the mouse if it could have been aware of the snake behind it with its mouth open wide. Soon, I confined myself to bed, praying that my quarantine would save me. And it's true, after a time, the thought that I'd become the mouse diminished. I knew it would. I knew if I'd isolated myself long enough the thought would fade, and I'd arrive at the truth.

How foolish I was to think I was the mouse. Of course, I was not the mouse. I was never the mouse. I was only one part in the great chain. There was the mouse, and behind the mouse the snake, and behind the snake there I was sitting in bed in my studio apartment afraid to open the door, afraid of what lie beyond the door waiting for me with its mouth open, waiting with all its desire bent on swallowing me whole.

THE HOLE

He didn't notice the hole until he was nearly finished painting. But there it was. A large hole in the middle of the wall, three feet by three feet. How could he not have noticed it? He approached the hole and peered through. On the other side lay a field of flowers where a bearded man lay naked, sleeping. What made it odd was that the hole should have led to his living room. Odder still was that the man's reddish-brown beard nearly covered his entire body like a blanket, shifting and shimmering as the man breathed. It looked almost as if it were alive. He reached his arm into the hole and touched the undulating blanket of a beard. Just as he suspected. Ladybugs. Thousands and thousands of ladybugs. He called to the man, but the bearded man didn't stir, not the slightest shift in his long, deep breaths. Breaths that made you feel as if you could float away on them. Breaths that could carry you to the cusp of clarity.

He tried to shake the man awake but only succeeded in attracting dozens of ladybugs to his own arm. He scooped one up with his index finger and studied its red shell, counted its spots. Seven. He flicked that one away and scooped another from his forearm. Seven spots again. He checked another, and another. Each one with seven dark, black spots atop that same blood-red shell. He scraped off the rest and watched as they scattered in all directions on the tarp he'd laid to catch the paint. His breathing stuttered. His chest clenched. He had a brief thought that perhaps he was having a heart attack. But no, there was no pain. Just a tightness in his chest. And those seven spots and that red shell. Why seven? Why so red? He found himself singing a nursery rhyme he'd learned as a child:

Ladybird, ladybird, fly away home
Your house is on fire and your children are gone
All except one, and that's Little Anne
For she has crept under the warming pan.

Where had that come from? And what happened to Little Anne? Nursery rhymes were never very nice. He ran to the closet, plugged in the vacuum and attached the turbo head to the multi-function hose before the bearded man had scarcely taken another breath.

Standing before the hole, holding the hose in his hand, he watched the ladybugs crawling and strutting over the man as if they owned him. He would let them know he was here. He. Was. Here. He turned on the vacuum and plunged the turbo head into the shimmering mass. They flew by the hundreds through the clear multi-function hose and into the belly of the vacuum.

There were so many he worried the machine might clog. But it kept dutifully sucking. Sucking. Normally frugal, he wouldn't have purchased a top-of-the-line vacuum, but something had compelled him, some premonition of this day, and he was thankful. For now he could see layers upon layers of ladybugs piling up in the clear plastic holding container. Returning with relish to the hole, he plunged the turbo head into the beard over and over again, alternating glances at the vacuum to monitor his progress.

It was only when the overfull vacuum sputtered and died, and he saw that the beard of ladybugs was still unchanged, that he began to panic. He took handfuls and handfuls of the little creatures and shoved them into the turbo head. But they just crawled out and over him. He brushed them onto the tarp. And that's when he saw it. The ladybugs had arranged themselves in seven large spots on the blood red tarp. When had the tarp turned red? It had been white, hadn't it? He was sure it had been white. Maybe the paint had spilled on it. But no, he'd been painting the walls taupe. Except that the walls of the room were also red. He could see that now. He'd been painting them red all along.

He took his brush and dipped it into the paint can, then painted over the ladybugs forming one of the spots on the tarp. He drenched them in paint, but it didn't matter because as soon as he'd moved to paint the

next spot, more ladybugs climbed on top of the painted bugs in the first spot, turning it a bottomless black
once again. He kicked the paint can over and watched
as the red paint slowly bled out over the ladybugs on
the tarp. He turned to the hole, watched the man lying
there deep in sleep, felt the man's breath sucking in and
out, in and out, as if the hole were a mouth. And now
the ladybugs were spilling out of that mouth. He had to
fill the hole, or at least cover it.

This time, he returned from the closet with duct
tape. Tirelessly, he stretched the tape back and forth
across the hole in long strips. Just one small patch left
to cover, and it would all be over. He tugged on the
roll of tape, but only a few more inches remained. Not
enough. Still, he applied it religiously, hoping somehow
it would do the job. When that failed, he slumped back
against the wall, head adjacent to the tiny hole that remained.

One by one the ladybugs crept out of the hole or up
from the tarp and onto his face, forming a long beard
that undulated over his body as he drifted in and out
of sleep dreaming of a hole he could fill in or cover up,
anything, so as never to disappear again.

I've hit the face of God head on. The rain falls and falls in the black night. The moon slivers white on the horizon. The highway a grey thread, unspooling. I sit in the car trying to talk to my wife as we return from an aborted dinner in the city. And there it is. Silver light bounding from the field. Silver light flashing through the air. A thud. Then the bump of tires rolling over something.

"What was that?" my wife asks.

"I have no idea," I reply, checking my rearview mirror. Nothing but the dark constellation of rain behind us.

"Should we stop? We should stop," she says, looking over her shoulder.

"It's too dangerous," I say. "If we stop, we'll be killed. Besides, it's dead or gone by now."

We pass the remainder of the drive guessing what it might have been.

"A deer," my wife says.

"Too easy," I reply. "Besides, that doesn't explain the flash of silver." The rain pounds the car. The wind howls outside. We sit in silence as each searches for the flicker of an answer. "A giant bunny!" I joke. "An escaped stormtrooper!" We laugh, happy that humor has jockeyed through the cracks of our fight at dinner.

"A refugee snowman!" my wife continues. "Don Johnson in his Miami Vice suit!" The last one nearly sends us off the road with laughter. But then a silence follows that neither of us has any idea how to handle.

My mind returns to the woman with whom I'd had an affair the year before, the woman whose ghost still haunts my marriage. The argument had gotten so heated at dinner, my wife had suggested that maybe it would have been better had I chosen to leave, to be with the other woman. *Just imagine what different lives we might be leading now,* she'd said. *What different people we might have become.* I sat for a long time staring at my steak after she'd said that, trying to imagine that life. *How do you know?* I asked. *What if we're just our same miserable selves but with a different person?* My wife took a long sip of her wine. When she looked at me, I couldn't tell if she hated or loved me. *I guess we'll never know,* she said, then excused herself to the bathroom.

When we arrive home, I run inside for a flashlight to examine the car. My wife stands in the doorway with the dogs, while I stand in the rain, panning the light across the bumper of the car. "I don't see anything," I start to say. "Wait! There's something here." My wife steps closer as we both examine the tuft of light grey hair caught in the seam between bumper and car. The hair is tinged with white and a hint of rust-colored red. The dogs push open the screen door and run wildly about the car, stopping and sniffing at the bumper but also beneath the tires, catching the scent of what must have been a coyote. The smell, so strong, so certain, it's difficult to pull them away.

That night I lie in bed thinking about the coyote. The beauty of its jump. The grace of that flash of silver in the night. How easy it was to love when the possibilities were endless. Now it's merely a tuft of hair stuck to a car, a scent I can't catch. The spirit never comes as we would have it. I close my eyes with the hope of sleep but it's slow to arrive. So slow that I'm not sure when it is that I find myself bounding across an open field, the stars splayed above me, the wind singing in my ear. Chased by rain, I run faster and faster until the darkness opens, and I see the road before me. I leap. Only then, as the wind carries me in its long arms do I understand its song.

True Sight

The squirrel had been there when he woke up for three days now. He knew it was still there, hanging upside down from his kitchen screen door, watching him with eyes so large they opened the night. He didn't have to look. He couldn't look. Not anymore. Not after the last time when he shuffled groggy-eyed downstairs from his bedroom wanting only that cup of coffee that promised to clear the unknown songs from his head. He'd tried to avoid seeing it then, as he'd tried the day before. But the squirrel skittered across the screen, upside down, always upside down, positioning itself close to the coffee pot, as close to him as it could get. It made him quite uncomfortable, as if the world were closing in on him. When he opened the back of the brewing machine to add the water, the squirrel let out a series of two chirps followed by what he could only describe as a bark. He didn't realize squirrels could bark like that, but then it did it again, and again. A series of two chirps and a bark. He tried to step away but found himself instead stepping closer, holding the pot before him like an offering. The squirrel went mad, running in circles on the screen, then figure eights, before again settling in its upside down position, staring at him with those large, dark eyes.

He comes because of me. He comes for me. The words burrowed into his mind. But where did they come from? And why was he now staring into those eyes unable to move. The squirrel twitched its nose and tail while it made a sort of ticking sound from deep within its belly. The man stood there hypnotized by that sound for how long he couldn't tell. Then the squirrel barked much louder than before. Much louder than he thought any animal could bark. He dropped the coffee pot. It shattered on the floor, scattering shards and water everywhere. And still he could not move. *He has broken free of the forest that wraps him,* the man thought, though it was not really a thought for it didn't come from his mind but ticked deep within his belly. Then he passed out. He woke to find he'd cut himself along the forearm and thigh. He must have landed on a couple of the shards. Blood mixed with water on the floor. The squirrel was gone. He disinfected and bandaged his wounds, then cleaned up the mess. Now he would be late for work.

On this day he avoided the kitchen altogether, bought his coffee at Starbucks before arriving at work as chief actuary for a large insurance company.

"Morning, Edgar. Morning, Chris. Morning, Joan," he said, without breaking his stride.

"Morning, Cass," they replied, eyes fixed on their own computer screens, bodies tight in their cubicles.

He liked working with the door to his office closed. The confined space allowed him to think, or so he told himself. Besides, he often grew annoyed hearing their small talk throughout the day. If they needed him, they could knock. And he had an important project to finish up—assessing a variety of risks related to insurance premiums for seniors. The boss had wanted his analysis yesterday but he hadn't been able to concentrate and was now behind for the first time in his career. Unfortunately, no matter how much of the bad office coffee he used to replenish his cup, the numbers wouldn't come together. He couldn't get a clear picture and that was his job. Was he getting enough sleep? He had been tossing and turning more than usual. Insomnia was not unknown to him. He remembered a long bout he'd had back in college when he'd failed one of his general ed requirements, a classics course on Greek myths, and it was uncertain whether or not he would graduate. How was he to know mythology wouldn't make any sense. Children sprouting out of thighs. Women turning into trees. Gods essentially raping any time they felt like it. Worst of all was the story of Agamemnon. Horrific. Children killing their mothers. Wives killing their husbands. How could you predict any of that? It all seemed so random. Of course, his worst bout of insomnia had occurred when he was ten. He didn't sleep for months after going hunting with his father.

It was the first time his father had taken him. They were supposed to be shooting pheasants. All he remembered now was the endless expanse of field and how cold it was, how all he wanted to do was go back and wait in the car as they trudged through the mud and weeds. His father carried a shotgun but had given him a twenty-two. As they walked, he recited to himself every detail his father had explained about gun safety, carrying the unloaded gun muzzle down. He'd had a feeling that somehow today was a test. And he was determined to pass.

So, when his father pointed out to him a squirrel in a maple not too far distant, he made sure to follow every step correctly as he loaded the gun. Neither he nor his father ever thought he'd actually hit the squirrel. It was more an exercise in loading and shooting. And you had to aim at something or what was the point? So when the squirrel dropped from the tree, Cass' mouth dropped as well. He forgot every rule of gun safety as he ran to the squirrel, rifle over his shoulder, pointed back at his father. He's thought many times since how lucky they were nothing more serious happened that day. The squirrel lay among the yellow and orange leaves, a hole ripped in its side, a tiny rivulet of blood trickling out. He remembered how surprised he was that he couldn't see any guts, the hole just opened to blackness, like there was nothing behind it. He remembered, too, reaching out to touch the hole, or wanting to anyway. Strangely, he couldn't remember if he did touch it or stick his finger inside. What caught his attention instead were the squirrel's eyes. The cloudy veil spreading across them like a shuttered room. A closed space he was trapped in. Of course, he couldn't have articulated any of that at the time. Only years later, when he thought about that day, would he come to even a glimmer of understanding. In that moment, all he could do was walk back toward the car, leaving the squirrel where it lay. He stayed by the car, shivering in the cold, until his father finally returned, annoyed that his son had ruined a good day of hunting. His father never asked him to go hunting again.

His office was always too hot in the fall. The company insisted on turning on the heat even though winter hadn't settled in. He loosened his tie and tried to deal with the stifling temperature by doubling down on his numbers. Only the more he tried to concentrate, the less the numbers came into focus. And the more the numbers lost focus, the more he began to sweat. He took off his jacket and rolled up his sleeves. That's when he heard the sound from somewhere beneath his desk. A ticking sound. Or rather a clicking, like the sound someone makes when they stick their tongue to the roof of their mouth and then release it quickly. He tried to ignore it at first but it only got louder.

It was here! The squirrel was somewhere in his office. He leapt from his chair, fighting off a feeling of panic that made him want to jump up on the desk. He'd make a fine sight if one of his team walked in. No. This was crazy. If a squirrel had gotten into his office, it wasn't *the* squirrel. It was just some random rodent. He grabbed the umbrella he always kept by the door in case of inclement weather and stabbed under the desk. Nothing. Slowly, he knelt and peered below. Still nothing. Then he heard the clicking sound again. But this time from somewhere above him, on the other side of the ceiling. Had the thing gotten into the vents? He opened his door.

"Joan, Edgar, you hear anything strange in the ceiling?" he shouted, forgetting he was still holding the umbrella like a sword.

Joan and Edgar gave each other a sidelong look from across their cubicles before answering in the negative.

"Chris, what about you?" Cass put the umbrella back in the stand by the door.

"Nothing, boss," Chris replied. He tilted his ear toward the ceiling. "Nope, don't hear anything. What's the matter? Think we have a mouse problem or something?"

"Yeah, maybe," Cass said, tapping the walls with his finger as if sounding them. "Maybe that's it." Then, in an attempt to regain his authority, he added. "Joan, why don't you call an exterminator. We don't want mice eating the phone lines."

He shut the door and tried to work, but it was no good. No matter how hard he tried, he couldn't make sense of the numbers. Clearly, he needed sleep. Maybe he'd call it a day and go home for a nap. Thankfully, when he arrived home the squirrel was not in its usual spot, hanging upside down from the kitchen screen door. In fact, the squirrel was nowhere to be found at all. Maybe he could get some rest. He laid his keys and wallet in the tray he'd placed on the shelf next to the microwave for exactly this purpose, then heated himself a glass of warm milk as had become his nightly habit and went upstairs for a nap. He laid his suit out on the small chair in the corner of the bedroom just as he would for his nightly routine, though this was only an afternoon nap. He took a last sip of his milk and got in bed, pulling the covers to his chin and tucking the sheet tightly about him on each side so that there was no empty space, something he used to do when he was a boy. He concentrated on controlling his breath, slowing it down so as to ease himself into sleep. Unfortunately, the more he tried to relax, the more he seemed to toss and turn. His legs grew jittery. His skin itched. He took the decorative pillows and lined them along each side of his body, walling himself in, then counted backwards from one thousand, thinking he might trick himself into sleep.

Just as he reached eight hundred and eighty-eight, the clicking sounded above his head. He opened his eyes to find the squirrel hanging upside down from the ceiling, staring at him, twitching its little nose and tail. It kept clicking like that, and the more it clicked, the more he felt sure he couldn't move, as if he were trapped in the coffin he'd made for himself. Then, just as it had done the day before while hanging from the kitchen screen door, it suddenly started barking. Loud, violent barks that would have made him jump, would have made him run from the bed if he would have been able to move. But try as he might, his body seemed locked in place.

Now the squirrel barked one long note sounded by two short ones. Its whiskers so close they tickled Cass' nose. It seemed angry with him. Its little teeth bared, face scrunched as if he gave off an awful stench. The barks grew louder and louder until all Cass could think about was covering his ears. He tried to move his hands, his legs, anything. But the more he struggled, the more entrapped he became, as if he was being held in a giant Chinese finger trap. His breath grew short. His eyes dimmed to pinholes. He was on the verge of panic when a pheasant flew past. And then another. He was no longer in his room but floating now above a cold field. A man and a boy walked below, the boy carrying his rifle as if it held his own death. The man pointed to something in a distant tree. The boy raised the gun, hesitated a moment, then pulled the trigger. Cass watched the boy approach the thing lying on the ground, as his father waited behind. Then everything went black, and Cass found himself looking up at the boy, as if he were the squirrel. The morning stars swelled around them, and the leaves, too, were shining. And for a moment, they shared a world without anguish or death. Then the boy's face changed, scrunching up, eyes shutting like a gate, fists clinching around the barrel of his gun. He knew then the boy was lost, torn from the souls rising from him like grass. That no matter how the boy tried to study the light tracing the curve along the banks of a river or the shadows purling across the branches of the trees at dusk, no matter what door opening to far-off ruins, he would never see clearly again.

The squirrel's barking shattered the vision, and he found himself looking up again at the whiskered face of some demented god. With each bark, the ceiling cracked. First just a small crack like the kind you get on your windshield when a pebble hits it. But then that crack grew. And as the squirrel kept barking, more cracks appeared, widening and splitting with each new bark. Soon, the ceiling was gone, opening to a dark void, an expanse from the middle of which the squirrel seemed to be floating upside down. The squirrel's head moved closer and closer until it hovered inches above Cass' face. He shut his eyes, but it didn't matter. The squirrel was still there, looking down at him from the center of all that blackness. He tried to shield his eyes with his hands, only now he wasn't sure he had hands or a body at all. He was no longer sure of anything except the barking that reverberated in his mind and the face of the squirrel that grew larger and larger. *Never more let me see you. Never more let me sleep and dream.* Again, words appeared, dug up from some deep place. Again, he tried to parse the meaning but couldn't break through. The more he turned the words around in his head, the less sense they made. And how could he concentrate anyway with the squirrel's face like a star, a great burning thing inches from his own face in the dark sky.

The mouth opened. His world became the dark hole of that opening, surrounded by its sharp, little teeth. He reached out to touch the opening, but his hand was not there. He looked down at his body but saw only empty space. He wanted to scream. He did scream and found himself floating on that scream into the dark chasm that was the squirrel's mouth.

The barking stopped. His screaming stopped, and everything was silent. The squirrel was gone. He was gone. Floating in darkness. Or perhaps, he was the darkness. The darkness that had been inside him all along. It didn't matter anymore. Nothing mattered. There was nothing he could do. He was dying. He felt sure of it. This was a heart attack, and he was having some form of delusion. What point was there in fighting? He relaxed. Took a deep breath and let go.

It felt like he was falling. That's the way he'd describe it later, at least the way he would describe it to himself as he wandered road after empty road. He would never tell anyone about this. Never. It felt like he was falling, though he couldn't be sure he was moving at all. There was nothing to measure the movement against. Only a swelling of the darkness that made it feel as if he were passing through something, a swelling and a shimmering.

And then it was over. He stood in the center of his yard beneath the morning sun, feeling its heat upon him. He studied his hands, his feet. He seemed to be whole again. He turned toward his house. There appeared to be someone on the other side of the sliding glass door that led to the kitchen. He walked toward the door and peered inside. His father stood before the coffee maker, busy making himself a cup, dressed in his orange hunting vest and camo cap. He looked as if he'd never aged. As his father reached for the carafe to fill his cup, a nut dropped from the ceiling and hit him on the head. His father didn't seem to notice. He continued pouring his coffee as first one and then another nut dropped on his head or into the coffee pot or his cup. Soon, nuts poured from the ceiling. All different kinds of nuts. Thousands and thousands of them falling on his father, flooding the kitchen, flowing out into the living room and up the stairs to the bedroom. Still, his father stood staring out the window, drinking his morning coffee.

Cass reached for the screen door. Touched it. Ran his fingers along the cage of fine metal tracings. He opened his mouth to say something, to shout a warning, but no words came out. And then he could no longer see his father, only nuts pressed floor to ceiling against the sliding glass door. A squirrel ran past his feet. Not *the* squirrel, though he couldn't be sure. It chirped at him then skittered away from the house, only to return and chirp again when it saw he didn't follow. The sliding glass door shattered under the pressure, nuts spilling onto the porch, piling higher and higher around him. The squirrel ran off. He fell to his knees under the weight of that unscalable solitude. Nuts and more nuts as far as he could see. He clawed at the dirt with first one hand and then another, digging up dirt as if with each handful he was gathering strength for what would follow. He had his work cut out for him in the coming winter.

Rumination

Last night I dreamed of a cow watching over me as I slept, it's large, wet eyes seeming to speak my fears of the coming day. In words that felt like silvery minnows in my mouth, I asked about monsters in the basement, ghosts in the attic, my son's hopes I'd folded and hidden in the junk drawer. He listened, though didn't answer, as if standing on the far side of a sun-blazed pasture, only partially aware of me. When I woke, I asked him for a magic bean. He turned from me as if to say this was not that kind of story. After I showered and dressed, I told him he may as well follow me to work. I didn't know he'd chew cud the whole time I sat at my desk. It made it difficult to get anything done. First he'd grind on the right side of his mouth, then the left. He appeared to swallow but the food kept coming back up. I remembered learning something about this as a child and googled—the food goes to the Rumen where it mixes with digestive juices and gets softer, then gets pumped back to the mouth. This process gets repeated, the next time going to the Omasum, then later the Abomasum. It's all so complicated I couldn't keep it straight. I watched the cow the better part of that afternoon as he stood there chewing. Most things in this world are hidden from us, I thought. Most things we don't see. The strange alchemy of a cow's stomach. The grief beneath whispered voices. The hurt beneath a son's downcast gaze. It was then I noticed that the cow was looking at me, had been watching in fact the entire time with the same wet eyes he'd turned on me in my sleep. I wondered then if I'd exhausted my cruelty.

That Hole is Everything

It wasn't the first time a boy had brought me home. But it would be the last. His eyes were gentle. The way he watched me, perhaps imagining the two of us together. His voice quiet, the way he whispered all the things he wanted to do with me. His hands kind, the way he gently traced his finger down the skin of my back before he scooped me up.

We spent the evening together in his garage. He watched as I hopped about looking for flies, snails, slugs. I was starving so really anything would do. Sometimes, he hopped about behind me, imitating every turn of my head, every croak that came from my mouth. I thought at first he was trying to communicate. Perhaps he was. There was a moment when he squatted before me croaking all sorts of nonsense when I could have sworn he said, "Help me from this body." Of course, he couldn't have known what he was saying. It was mere coincidence. You know what they say, *If you give a chimp a typewriter . . .*

We could have gone on like that all night, and if we had, maybe we could have bridged the gulf between us. Who knows what's possible, really? I certainly never could have imagined what happened instead. You probably won't believe me either by the time I finish my tale. But it's true. Every word of it. His mother called him in for bed. At first he didn't go. But then his father called, too. He crouched down beside me and tickled my back with his forefinger. I didn't know interspecies love could feel so good. "Don't go away," he said. "Please don't go away. I'll be back in the morning." I croaked back that I'd be happy to spend the night if he could bring me a small tub of water. I didn't need much. He stood and made his way to the door, then stopped, his eyes catching the glint of something shiny on the shelf. For a moment, I thought he'd understood, but then he grabbed what was apparently an old coffee can and, before, I could say or do anything, ran back and placed the can over me. "Now, you can't leave!" he said. "And we'll play together all day tomorrow!"

I wasn't prepared for the darkness. It sounds like a ridiculous statement. We, toads, are mostly nocturnal, but this was different. The darkness was so thick I was afraid it would choke me. I waved a webbed foot to swat at it and felt instead as if the darkness had swallowed my foot. Fear nearly crippled me. Not the fear of impending death. But rather the fear that I would have to live like this forever, alone. Death, by contrast, seemed welcome. It's strange how the mind works. After that brief period of paralyzing fear, I became calm. I knew with a certainty I'd rarely felt before that forever would only be a matter of hours. I could feel my skin drying up. The inside of my mouth turned to cotton. I don't know when exactly during the night I slipped clear of my body. I only know that I did.

It's difficult to describe what happened next. I was still in the coffee can, and yet I was not. Or rather, it was as if the space inside the coffee can expanded to include all that was outside as well. The insufferable weight of darkness was gone. Yet it was still dark. But now the darkness was like a kiss, a kiss that opened to another world. The nearest thing I can think of is that feeling you get when you immerse yourself again in water after a long day in the open air. That feeling of dreaming while awake. At which point, I was a tadpole wiggling through the murk. At which point, I was old, half-buried in mud, wanting only for the day to end. At which point, the chorus of croaks from my home pond became a city of tears. At which point, I staggered forth from my tiny corner of this fallen world. At which point, I was no longer alone.

The boy burst through the door shortly after sun-up and bound through the garage, beaming. Then, he picked up the coffee can and froze. His face changed. Not puffed out as we do when we see a predator but the opposite, as if it caved in. He sat on the cement and slowly, carefully reached his finger toward the dried-out husk. Almost as if he were afraid of it, he tapped the shriveled shape with his finger. He tried moving it, and when it didn't respond, he hit it away, covering his own face with his hands. He sat there like that a long time, his whole body shaking as if in that moment he wanted nothing more than to escape it, to finally rid himself of it. If I could have, I would have scooped him up and carried him home, the same as he'd done for me. I would have reminded him that at the end of life there is a hole, and that hole is everything. I would have said that I believe those holes are connected. I would have done that, but in this upside-down dream of a world the voice with which you cry is no longer your own and the ears with which you might hear anything that could make a difference make their own squall, like an ocean that keeps on breaking.

That Which Does Not Kill Us

I'm fifty-six. I've seen death. I've seen betrayal. I once held a mother as she cried, begging God to kill her child and spare him from the torment he suffered due to OCD. But in all my life, I've never seen someone as sad as the ten-year-old girl I met when I was not much older, the girl whose cat had just hung itself by its leash on the picket fence edging our park. A Calico. She'd taken it for a walk before dinner. She told me she'd used the leash because she didn't want it to get away. But of course it did. By the time she'd found it, the cat was already dead. It must have climbed the fence, and when it jumped down, the leash got caught. I wandered by five minutes later and found her there, on her knees, before the cat.

She was afraid of what her parents would do, so I offered to help. We wrapped it in a towel with daisies. My sister's favorite. I'd also grabbed a shovel and my grandmother's rosary from my home, which I found tucked away in Grandma's bedside table. She'd been staying with us for the past year. My mother said her mind was going. As it turned out, she only had a few months more.

We tried digging a hole in the grass of the park where the cat had died, but either the ground was too hard, or I was too weak. So we went to the field behind the elementary, an area I knew well. I found a soft place at the bottom of a gully and dug the hole. It was much easier than I thought.

I was surprised when she placed the cat in the ground herself. I don't know if I could have done that. I know that when my grandma passed months later, I could barely bring myself to peek into the casket. I set the rosary on top of the cat, then shoveled the dirt over it. We made a cross from two sticks and my shoelace. The girl and I stood there staring at the mound of freshly turned earth. "It seems like there's something more we should do," the girl said. "Isn't there more?"

I thought about the night two weeks before when I prayed for the first time. I'd said ten "Our Fathers" and ten "Hail Mary's," as my grandma had taught me to do, because I had a test in math the next day that I'd forgotten to study for. I prayed for something to happen, and though God didn't answer that night, the next day, the teacher was sick. No test. I'd been a believer ever since. And so I prayed again, even harder than before. I said my ten "Our Fathers" and ten "Hail Mary's" and then added one more for good measure. I talked about how I'd never seen a girl as sad as this, about how I'd never felt feelings like this before. I didn't understand most of the feelings at the time, but the longer I stood there praying with that girl crying beside me, the longer I stood waiting for something to happen, the angrier my voice became, and some of that rage crept into my words. I don't remember what I said. Or perhaps, I didn't even know then. All I know is that when I was done, I turned, only to see the girl's back as she walked away.

Over four decades have passed since then, and I've rarely if ever thought about that girl. To tell the truth, I find it difficult to concentrate on anything anymore. Or even to leave the house. It's all I can do to get up and force myself through the day. I smile. I go through the motions. No one in my family seems to notice. However, a few days ago, the ghost of her cat appeared. It started with a few random sightings. I'd see something move out of the corner of my eye, something jumping down from the sofa, or running around the corner. I knew it was a cat, maybe even a Calico, but I didn't know it was *that* Calico until I followed it to my bedroom and found the rosary. My grandma's rosary on the hardwood floor. The same chip in the cross near Christ's foot. I asked my wife and kids if they'd seen the cat, but they just stared as if I was crazy.

The next morning after my wife went to breakfast, the cat sat at the foot of my bed, watching me.

"I don't understand," I said. "Why me? Why aren't you haunting the girl?"

The cat turned its head and licked its armpit.

"Why now?" I asked, inching closer. "Why after forty-four years?" This time, the cat yawned, then curled up on the bed near my feet. I suppose I shouldn't have expected an answer.

Grief lays down parallel paths. It's one of the few things I've learned. Forty years ago, there was the cat and my grandma. And now the cat was back. Did this signal another grief, one I was not yet aware of, or one I'd forgotten, maybe even suppressed? You see, one of the other things I've learned is that the things that break us aren't always big. Sometimes, they're so small we don't see them at all, until it's too late. Deaths. Betrayals. Divorces. Those are easy to spot, so at least we can attempt to deal with them. It's the other moments—the small exhalation of disappointment when a friend doesn't return a call, the false promise of the sun on a day strewn with dark arrows, the disgust on your daughter's face when you say the wrong thing, or how your wife turns away to check her cell as you tell her about your promotion. These moments accumulate with a quiet power until they become bigger than the biggest of griefs. That's what the appearance of the ghost cat made me think of now. I'd had more than my share of those things. We all do.

The next morning when the cat appeared, I opened the front door and waited. He hesitated, looking up at me, then out the door at the blue sky beyond, then behind him, as cats do. "If you're not ready yet, that's fine," I told him. He turned away and walked back to my bedroom, where I found him once again curled on the bed. The next day, I tried a different tact, encouraging him to jump up on the back of the armchair in the living room and look out the window. It had the same result. My wife and kids watched me opening the door or standing before the window. They may have even heard me talking to the ghost cat. But if they did, it didn't register. Or at least they didn't say anything.

"You didn't get much of a life," I said to the cat as he licked his paws the following morning on my bed. It was a Saturday, and my wife was out gardening.

The cat looked at me, then looked at its back, as if it might clean that, too.

"I'm talking to you." I said. "Can't you hear me?"

The cat blinked once or twice, then rested its head on its paws. Something about its nonchalance bothered me. The way it didn't seem to care what I did. The way whatever I did didn't make a damn bit of difference.

I kicked it off the bed. It howled, then jumped back on.

I rose and opened the window, the cool air like water over my skin. There was a rapid sound of hammering outside. A small machine-gun in my brain.

"I bet you can't name that bird," I said, pointing out the window to the woodpecker sitting atop the picket fence at the back of our yard.

The cat looked at me and blinked, then rolled on its back and cleaned its belly.

"You don't even see it, do you?" I shouted. "You're here for no reason. Just roaming around this house, licking yourself!"

The cat yawned and gave me a side-look.

"It's a woodpecker," I screamed. "A fucking red-crested pileated woodpecker!"

I punched out the window screen. "Here, let me help you!" I shouted. "It's easy, see!"

The screen fell to the porch with a crash, startling my wife weeding in the yard. She stepped away from me until it almost looked like she'd fallen backward into a sky scrubbed of clouds. "Hail Mary, full of grace . . ." I muttered beneath my breath.

The cat jumped off the bed and walked out of the bedroom, into the the hallway beyond.

"You son-of-a bitch!" I shouted after it, "Get back here!" I stomped down the hall after it. "I'm not through with you yet. Do you hear me?" Patterns of light and dark checkerboarded the hall.

A faint scratching. At first I thought it was the cat, but then it sounded like hundreds, maybe thousands, of little mice in the walls. I steadied myself against the frame at the intersection with the kitchen corridor. There it was—the silhouette of the cat half-stained with sunlight from the kitchen, half in darkness, sitting there, flicking its tail.

"Just tell me where to go," I pleaded. "What to do next?"

And then the cat was gone. More than gone. It was as if it had never been. The scratching from the walls increased in volume, like the promise of everything I'd ever desired rising up about me, a wave washing through the darkening hallway. I sank to the hardwood floor and tried to call out after my wife, but my tongue was like a knife in my throat. The more I yelled, the more it cut, until my mouth filled with blood to match the blood pounding in my ears. So this is what it meant to be alone.

Words are Made for Ministration

He hates walking his dog after rain. It's not the puddles or toweling off his dog after. Or even that his dog licks the dew off each blade of grass instead of peeing so he's late for work. It's the earthworms. They're everywhere. He can't think about anything except where to step. It's inevitable he'll step on one. Take this morning. He let his guard down. The tiniest fraction. Thinking of his father, the fact that he didn't pass the memory test at the doctor's the other day. "He blew it," his mother had said. He'd noticed his father forgetting things, losing track of the conversation, then starting up a "new" conversation about something they'd talked about the day before. He'd been fearing this moment. Both his father's parents had suffered horribly from Alzheimer's. So, he knew it was a matter of time. Last night, he'd gotten angry with his father. "You've told me that story three times in the last week, Dad!" His father got quiet after that, and there was nothing he could do to salvage the moment.

He stepped on the earthworm just as he recalled that conversation. A big one. Eighteen inches long and as thick as his finger. It wrapped around his foot the second he stepped on it. He kicked it off, sending it to the edge of the road near the grass, where it writhed uncontrollably. His dog lurched for it, but he held him back, his dog pulling at the leash, trying to get at it, whimpering. But he didn't leave. He couldn't stop staring at it. The way it twisted and turned, flipped and flopped, as if an alarm inside had sounded and now wouldn't turn off. How it couldn't stop even after the middle of it had been squashed, making of escape its torture. He wanted to ask forgiveness. He didn't know where the impulse came from, and yet he couldn't do it. The best he could do was stand there and watch.

The problem was it wouldn't quit, as if it didn't know what had happened, didn't understand. It kept trying to move, trying to go about its journey across the road to some drier patch of land. And the best he could do was wait. For what he wasn't sure. Maybe, a word. A word yet to be invented. A word that might take back what seemed promised. A word that might redeem everything. But the longer he stood there waiting, wishing for that word and then, perhaps, dare he think it, maybe another, the more he wondered if it would ever come.

A Violent Storm
After Muso Soseki

When the mind is still, the air I fly in becomes endless space. That's what I tell myself anyway. It's part of the new me. The old me sat in that hard shell under the ground counting the seconds until I could pupate, until I could be free of that god-awful space. Everything hurt cramped like that. My left wing kept falling asleep and both antennae were bent in half. I never thought they'd be straight again. I also thought it would be easier above ground. I was wrong. Flying around all night sending out a Morse code of light, just waiting for any female to signal back. An exercise in futility.

With compassionate wings, Buddha saves those who are lost. That's another one I tell myself. I figure if I keep saying it, maybe eventually it will be true. Maybe eventually I'll believe.

And then it happens, a flash of light from across the distance. I don't move at first. I simply hover there above the grass. It can't be real. After so long, a light as big and beautiful as that can't be for me. I play my own concerto of luminescence, my cry for love, then wait for what seems like an eternity. It happens again, that big, beautiful flash of light beaming from behind the azaleas. I rush forward and fly right into an invisible wall. Before I know it, I'm trapped inside some sort of see-through cell, a giant eye looking back at me. A human eye. I've seen creatures like this before running through the grass with us. Sometimes they'd try to catch us in their hands. But this one was the first to use our light against us. She was smart.

"Mom! Dad! It worked!" she shouts as she runs into her nest. What I can only assume is her father sits in front of a glowing box that seems to have hypnotized him. Her mother sits opposite, holding what looks like a collection of thin leaves. She turns one over and stares at it. Neither of them look up.

"I talked to the fireflies! I flashed a light and got one to come to me!" No response. The girl gives a sort of snort, then heads to her room, setting me on the table near where she sleeps, before leaving to go I know not where. Thank God she'd had the foresight to punch air holes in my prison. I'd heard stories of others who'd met a fate like this. We called them "The Disappeared." Serves me right, I thought. A fitting end to a wretched and meaningless life. I should have known better than to ever think the sky would be better than my cramped existence below ground. If you could call that an existence.

The girl returns with a collection of leaves much like the one her mother was holding. "Did you know that your light is the most efficient in the world?" she says, eyes ablaze. "You're lucky I found you," she adds. "It says here that there's another species that pretends to be a female, then eats you when you come to mate. That's gross!" She doesn't have to tell me. Life so far has been one long string of disappointments.

I flash my light over and over, saying, "There's not enough air. I can't breathe!" or "For the love of God, open the lid!" But all I get for my trouble are those big blue eyes pressed up against the glass, a smile on her face, like she actually believes existence isn't simply a joke. This goes on until her parents peek their heads in the door and tell her to go to sleep.

The night is long and dark. I keep flashing frantically, and the girl keeps smiling and watching me, even as she drifts off. Sometime after midnight, I collapse in exhaustion.

The next morning, the girl carries me with her wherever she goes, setting me next to her as she eats what appears to be some sort of corn floating in cow pee, then in another room as she rubs a stick with hairs on it up and down in her mouth, and later still as she hunts outside for flowers to decorate my prison. At least I can be thankful my captor's an astute scholar. I won't starve. It's exhausting, being carted around like that with no shade to hide in. I barely have strength enough to resume my attempts at communication when night falls. I try every sequence I can think of, mixing in a smattering of words I've picked up from other species in the hope that one will connect. All I get are those adoring blue eyes and the occasional, "What are you trying to say now, cutey?"

A couple days later, and I don't even get that. I didn't know how good I'd had it. I sit on her bedside table as she goes out to play. When she returns at night and I beam with every bit of light I can muster, I scarcely get a glance. A week later, just before bed, her mother moves me to the dust covered top of her bookshelf. My life just keeps moving from bad to worse.

I panic. I fly against the glass walls of my prison again and again. If I can't escape, at least maybe I can end it all. But like so much of my pathetic existence, I fail at that, too, falling to the flower strewn jar-bottom, semi-conscious. I don't know how long I remain that way. Days. Weeks. Months. Years. I may as well be back in that hard case in the ground. The irony is not lost on me. I've come full circle. And that's when it hits me. My own voice speaking to me from the past. *When the mind is still, the air I fly in becomes endless space.* What a fool I'd been. I had it all wrong. It wasn't about escaping to the open air, but the opposite. *This jar must feel ashamed to be so small.* My voice again, speaking to me now, though I don't understand at first. Perhaps it's delirium from the concussion I've probably induced. Or perhaps it's all a dream. But then the voice speaks again. My voice. Strong and fierce as if nothing had ever happened to it. *In this small jar are worlds beyond number.* I force myself upright, my head still spinning, and I fold my four lower legs into a lotus position, resting my two front legs on top, claws making a Dhyana Mudra in my lap. I sit in the center of the jar and relax my mind. I watch each panicked thought float through it. I see myself rise above the flowers and out the air holes in the lid. I see the open window before me, the hole in the screen big enough for a moth to fit through. I see the lights blinking on and off, beckoning. I see the jar below me. The dust from the bookshelf rises in a violent storm, swirling about me like a chrysalis.

THE UNTELLING

It happened when I was wheeling the trashcans out to the curb before taking the children to school. I almost ran face-first into it, a mantis caught in a web dangling from the top of the garage door. A small circle of light, spreading around it from the rising sun. I don't know if there was a breeze, or if it was my own breath, or the wind from my passing so close, but the mantis spun round and round in the web, each pass of its iridescent eyes reflecting worlds countless as dust, and in each world, a different path home.

The dog barked. My husband stood in the doorway, shouting that we were late, unaware of the terrifying beauty dangling just a few feet before him. I was alone with the fire of its eyes, unable to turn away until my children rushed past, grabbing my hand and yanking me from my spot. The sky stayed blue, but everything else changed. Or perhaps I had changed. It was difficult to know. My daughters seemed like my daughters, singing *Scooby-Doo* in the backseat. My husband seemed like my husband, talking on and on about a new fitness club he wanted to join as he sat beside me. I heard them, and yet it was as if they were speaking to me from deep inside an endless maze. "Mommy, can we go to a sleepover at Kylee's?" And my husband's curt response. "You know you're not old enough yet to do that." "When will be old enough?" they pleaded. "Never, if I get my way," I said, surprising both my husband and myself. I laughed and so did the kids. My husband shot me a look. After I'd dropped them off, I wasn't sure they'd been there at all.

Instead of driving to work, I returned home. The mantis spun back and forth in the web. Dead. Had it been dead before? I couldn't remember. When I tried to recall it, all I could see were its eyes, the little black spots at their center like tiny black holes, each its own universe, watching me. They watched me still. *Everything will outlast you,* I thought. Or was it the mantis speaking to me again?

"Why are you crying?" my daughters asked, when they returned home on the bus. Again, I had no answer. They took my hand and led me into the house. Gave me a glass of lemonade, then went upstairs to play. I drank the lemonade and felt much better. I began to think it had all been one of those things. The kind of moments that seem significant but really have more to do with being dehydrated or overly tired. I decided I'd spend the rest of the afternoon playing with my daughters but couldn't make it up the stairs for all the webs that kept getting in the way, clinging to me, sticking to my fingers, my hair.

I went back outside, but the mantis was gone, only

a few tendrils of torn web remained dangling from the garage door. I listened to the faintness of my breathing, the fragility of it. I wondered what had happened to the mantis, those eyes. That night, I went to bed early, put on my silk negligee and waited. My husband came in after watching TV as usual. He talked and talked, assuming I heard every word. I had no idea what he was saying, only that some moments change everything. Some moments make it so that your eyes burn open. Then nothing anyone can say or do will bring back the person you once were. When my husband climbed into bed, I climbed on top of him. "Well this is a pleasant surprise," he said. As I worked him with my hand, his face multiplied before me. The effect was dizzying.

He kissed me. I'm not sure if I kissed him back. Soon, I couldn't see him at all. It didn't matter if my eyes were open or closed, all I could see was the strand of web wrapping itself about me, stretching out from my torso to the bedroom door, then down the hall and out through the garage and across the street. The strand worked its way through trees and over bushes as it wound about the playground, then across the fields behind our subdivision. At the other end, I was not surprised to see the mantis dangling, spinning there alone with the sound of everything I would ever lose.

After we made love, she begged me not to impale myself on her fangs. I thought I'd make it easy for her. You know. Avoid the mess, not to mention a scene. But she wouldn't hear of it. She wanted me to take up running again, said she loved the way I sprinted across the bathroom floor at the first sign of trouble. When I thought of running, I thought of disappearing. I didn't tell her that. Better to be daggered and mourned. I threw myself at her. But she knocked me away with her pedipalps and called me a coward. I crept to the other side of the web. Counted flies until I could sleep. When morning came, I wasn't any better off. She was still there, if anything, bigger than before, as if she'd found her purpose and sucked the life out of it to nourish her own. She'd always had that kind of clarity. And I, well, let's just say, yesterday marked the first real decision of my life. It should have been my last. Slowly, careful not to make the slightest vibration, I tight-roped off the web and down to the floor, away from her. If she wouldn't kill me, I'd do it myself. But just as I stepped toward the white whirlpool where I'd seen so many leave this world, the two-legged giant who terrorizes our home opened the door, showering our web with light. I froze. My eight eyes panning from the whirlpool to her and back again. The linear path of death or the tangled odyssey of love. The shimmer of gold refracted off the labyrinthine web, and for a fleeting moment, I saw my path outlined like a poem.

The Persistence of Spiders

Green and blue dragonflies flitted about the potted plants and flowers on Raymond's deck. A three-foot cocoon filled with wriggling worms weighed down several branches of the only tree in the back yard, a weeping willow. Raymond had called an exterminator to destroy the cocoon and a tree doctor to save the tree; he still wasn't sure what sort of worms were ravaging it, and he wouldn't know for another few months whether the tree would survive. But the cocoon and the dragonflies were nothing compared to the spiders, which were monstrous, their webs everywhere, enshrouding bushes, and cordoning off entire sections of the deck.

Raymond wondered at what point he had lost control. Before moving to Boulder, he and his wife, Carol, had been living in a late nineteenth-century Dutch Colonial in central Denver. They'd called it the barn because it required constant repair. Raymond hated it. Early on, his "Honey Do" list stretched across the fridge, and Raymond seemed incapable of shortening it. He wanted a new home with sparkling bathroom chrome, the smell of fresh Berber carpeting in the air. Carol acquiesced, hopeful that the new house would mark a change in her husband.

"Things will be better now," Raymond said the day after they'd made an offer on the house.

"New houses have problems too," Carol replied. Then added, "But I like the four bedrooms."

"What do you mean by that?" Raymond asked, moving to the kitchen.

"Nothing." Carol followed, staying close behind him.

"We bought it because of the lot, not the bedrooms," he said, filling a glass from the purifier on the fridge, then downing it in one gulp. He turned to his wife. "And we've had this discussion before. Things are perfect."

They'd moved into the house in May, when the flowers in the yard were all cheerful reds and happy yellows, and the weeping willow didn't sag quite so much. But now it was mid-July and the flowers had shriveled; the tree, defeated by the worms, looked as if it didn't care whether it lived or died. The sprinkler system had ruptured, causing the basement to flood, and a crack had appeared along the ceiling in the master bedroom.

The house backed up to what Raymond had thought was a forest but turned out to be a swamp. He cursed himself for not looking over the backyard fence to see the stagnant water covered with a yellowish-green growth and the ground that seemed to writhe and shift at twilight. The night after they'd moved in Raymond stood on the back deck grilling Mahi Mahi soaked in ginger sauce, staring worriedly at the long branches of the cottonwoods that hung like fingers into his back-yard. He imagined snakes dropping from the branches, slithering their way into his house. The high-pitched screams of two raccoons fighting somewhere beyond the perimeter of his yard so unhinged him that he brought in the Mahi Mahi slightly undercooked.

"Kids would love it here," Carol said over dinner. "Adventures right out the back door!"

Raymond picked at his food, the dinner's failure still bothering him, then laughed, a sound more like a sigh. "Some of my best memories are of catching bugs and lizards with my dad, in the fields behind my house when I was a kid."

"You never told me that." Carol gave him a warm smile. Raymond studied his fork. "There was a ravine that stretched for miles through the fields. On weekends, during the summer, we never left that ravine." He set the fork down. "Carol?"

"Yes."

He took a deep breath but couldn't bring himself to say anything.

Raymond was co-founder of a magazine called *Civitas*, dedicated to the creation of healthy communities. He arose each day at six, did a half-hour of yoga, made himself a latté, then went to work in his study, writing articles for the magazine—and, since the magazine only had a circulation of a few thousand, occasionally publishing articles in venues that paid better. The articles gave him a certain amount of notoriety, and he was often asked to speak in political and social policy forums. His specialty involved structuring communities based on the interdependent relationships in nature. The speaking engagements paid well, and though he believed in what he had to say with the zeal of a minister, it was the feeling he had when he stood before those rooms of policy makers that drove him, the feeling that he could shape the world any way he saw fit.

"The basic principles of ecology are obvious," Raymond said to Carol over coffee one afternoon a month after they moved in. "Nothing is isolated—everything in nature is part of a vast, intricate system."

"And when something new is introduced?"

He loved that she tried to test him. "The beauty of nature is that it maintains equilibrium no matter what factors are introduced."

"So babies don't upset the balance?"

"No," Raymond said, caught off guard. "That's different." He shifted his latté from one side of the table to the other before taking a sip.

"How?" Carol leaned in close.

"Well," Raymond stammered, searching for a gesture, a slight upturning at the corner of her mouth that would reveal it all as a joke. "Well, don't you see?" he said, finally. "Don't you see? It has a purpose within a greater system. Every niche has a purpose."

"Like what? What are you saying?" She tapped her fingernails on the tabletop.

"Offspring continue that…" He couldn't think with the noise her fingers were making.

"Offspring?" Carol interrupted. "You mean a baby? You mean when someone has a child?"

"Stop it," Raymond exclaimed, looking about him to see if anyone was staring. "I'm talking about something else."

"You're always talking about something else," Carol said, rising, preparing to leave.

"Don't you see that in a human society there's no system of checks and balances?" He reached out to her.

"What are you talking about, Ray?" You sound like a textbook. Talk to me. To *me*." She sat down again.

A couple at the next table watched them. Ray looked down at his latté, speaking into the table. "It's not that simple, Carol."

"Bullshit!" Carol said without lowering her voice.

Raymond paused, whispering. "Over long periods of time stasis is maintained…"

"Bullshit!"

Raymond's face went white. He used to enjoy these conversations. She used to offer suggestions to help with his articles. "Please don't talk like that."

"I'll stop, if you'll stop."

Sitting in his swivel chair late the next morning, Raymond stared past his computer. A large spider web hung from the underside of the deck in front of his study window. It hadn't been there the day before; he was sure of that.

An hour went by, and Raymond didn't move. He wanted to see the creature that could make a web like that. Even the largest of the other webs in the yard were only a fraction of the size of this one, and it glistened as if alive. Raymond clicked on the Internet and searched for spiders.

All spiders produce venom that is poisonous to their normal prey...Venom is injected through the hollow fangs to immobilize the prey...Some spiders use web snares to trap prey, and all construct a silk sac to deposit eggs.

Fifteen minutes passed. A housefly flew into the center of the web. Raymond could almost hear its frantic buzzing as it tried to extricate itself, the little wings beating against the constricting snare. He waited for the spider to attack. Nothing. He continued to stare out the window. He went back to the Internet to determine what type of spider could make a web that big. The *Orb Weaver* was the closest, but its webs were only a few feet in diameter. Another fifteen minutes passed, and another bug became caught in the web—this time a wasp. He wondered why the spider wasn't rushing out as it was supposed to do.

Taking a broom from the kitchen, Raymond went outside to destroy the web. Two dragonflies darted past, chasing each other. He swatted at them. Descending the deck stairs to the porch below, he noticed a small, black spider, about a half-inch in diameter, with orange spots, spinning a web between the deck and the stair rail. Raymond took a batter's stance and knocked the spider across the yard. The action felt great, but instead of a smile, Raymond's face took on a morose aspect; his eyes held a heaviness that gave him the look of a man preparing for battle.

He approached the monstrous web under the deck, but the spider was nowhere to be seen. Raising the broom in the air, he destroyed in a few seconds what the spider had taken all night to build. Elated, Raymond scraped off thick strands of web from the broom with his shoe, left the broom outside, and returned to his study.

The article he was writing was entitled "Persistence: The first Step Towards a Healthy Community." *Nature eradicates change.* That was the opening line. *Over time, anomalies, disturbances and decay are incorporated into the community. Nature's persistence can be modeled in our own communities. Let us be as constant as the ph of the oceans!*

Afterwards, he went for a jog and showered. There was still time to make dinner before Carol came home.

"I don't even want to know how big that spider was." Carol shivered as she sat at the dinner table, sipping her wine.

"We probably won't now," Raymond said, dabbing at his lips with the napkin. "So, what did you think of the meal?"

"It was a nice surprise," Carol said. "Thank you." And she raised her wine glass to toast. "Here's to working things out."

"You bet."

"I just want us to be happy."

"We are happy." Raymond stabbed the last red pepper on his plate with his fork, then rose to clear away the plates.

"Let me do that," Carol said, rising before him. "You sit down and relax."

Raymond moved to the living room to sip his wine and stare out the bay window into the twilight sky. The cottonwood branches swayed in the breeze, the leaves taking on darker shades of blue or bruised purples within the green. One branch stood out from the rest, leafless, emerging from the imminent darkness. Something about the branch frightened him, and he gulped his wine down. By the time Carol joined him, the drink had had its effect.

"You have beautiful eyes," he said. "Your dark hair sets off the blue."

Carol settled into an armchair opposite him. "Thanks," she said. "You haven't said that in a long time." She pulled her legs up under her. "You look pretty good yourself today. Did you go running?"

Raymond imagined his hand gently touching her legs, caressing her knee and moving up under her dress. "Why don't we do it?" The suddenness of the words surprised him.

"What do you mean?"

"You know."

"What? Have a baby?"

"Yes," he said, rising. He walked to the window, opened it and inhaled the night air. "Yes," he said again. "Let's have a baby!"

After, Carol went upstairs to shower, and Raymond went out to the deck. Switching on the floodlight, he stood within its beam, thankful for the fact that the intensity of the light effectively shut out the trees in the darkness beyond. He took a deep breath and relaxed, but something brushed against his face. Waving away a trace of web, he saw a small, gray and brown spider hanging from the floodlight behind his head. He grabbed the broom, but when he turned around the spider was gone.

He went inside but couldn't close the sliding door behind him. The frame had warped because of the settling of the house, and now the door was stuck in its track an inch short of closing. "Damn it!" Raymond barked. "How can it be fine one minute and broken the next!"

August and much of September came and went with no sign of the giant spider or its web. The leaves yellowed, as if anticipating an early winter. The house remained in relatively fine order, although the disposal broke when Raymond unknowingly dropped a washcloth into it. The repairman arrived promptly, and Raymond watched in envy as he crawled beneath the sink.

"I've never been much of a fixer-upper," Raymond said.

"Well, luckily these new houses don't have many problems."

"My line of work is public policy," Raymond continued. "My father was a handyman. He tried to train me, but I could never be like him."

"Yeah," the repairman said, his head still immersed beneath the sink.

"Not that I ever wanted to be," Raymond said, leaning against the counter.

"I know what you mean," the repairman said. "When I left home, I got as far away from the old man as I could."

"You want some water," Raymond said. "I'm feeling a bit thirsty."

Late September was Raymond's favorite time of year: not too hot, not too cold. He only hoped that when the leaves fell from the trees hanging over his back fence, there wouldn't be many. He wasn't worried about the weeping willow; it was already dead. Then, one Sunday morning, Raymond woke to find Carol cleaning out the closet in the guest bedroom.

"You want to go for a bike ride along the creek?" he asked.

"I want to get this room cleaned out," Carol replied. "Do you think we can get some paint? I'd like to get it painted this weekend."

"I was thinking we could head up to the mountains tomorrow, maybe still catch the leaves changing," Raymond replied.

"What do you think of a sky-blue color? That's neutral isn't it?" She said, staring at the ceiling.

"This is all in preparation for later, right?" He reached out, ran his hand along the wall.

"Raymond, I thought you were excited about this."

"Blue, would be nice," he said. "Maybe we could even stencil in some clouds or a tree."

***

The next morning the web was back, stretched between the pillars on the underside of the deck, almost blocking access to the grill on the cement porch. It glistened in the morning dew, a challenge of perfected beauty. A large green dragonfly was caught near the outer rim, its head missing. It couldn't be from the same spider, Raymond thought, not after nearly two months.

He went outside and grabbed the broom, then studied the victim. Its translucent wings shimmered as if it were still alive. Below the gaping hole where the head should have been, one of the legs twitched.

That night Raymond couldn't sleep. Rather than wake Carol, he thought he'd go down to his study to do some work. He passed the guest bedroom before descending the stairs, and, compelled by a need he didn't understand, entered, turning on the light. The blue color really was pretty, he thought. And the clouds had turned out well. He'd done them himself, and now he sat down on the floor to admire them. This was the next step in life, wasn't it? It was time to move beyond himself, and what better teacher than a baby.

The closet door, slightly ajar, caught his attention. Inside, a "Peter Rabbit" mobile lay atop blankets of various colors. He picked up a yellow one and rubbed it against his face. He would wrap their baby in that blanket, holding him in his arms while he sang him to sleep. Funny, he hadn't realized he wanted a boy. Still, it didn't matter what the baby was, he thought; he would teach it to read, he would teach it everything he knew: how the refraction of light makes the sky blue, or how the salt water of the oceans is the same concentration as in our bodies. I'll be a good father, he thought.

Three pairs of tiny socks lay beside the blankets. He picked up a pair and stuck his finger in one, shocked at the size. Bringing it to his face, he inhaled, taking in the moth breath of air. So small. He sat there holding the socks, the blanket lying over him, and imagined the two of them, father and son, exploring the wetlands behind the house. *Why did you lie about your father hunting bugs and lizards with you in the field?* He hadn't lied, had he? He'd remembered it clearly, had always remembered it that way. No. It was a lie. His father had barely been around, driving from one plains state to another, selling ink. When his father was home he was cold and aloof. He'd been valedictorian at his high school graduation, but his father didn't even show up. Said he had to paint the house. Raymond twisted the tiny sock around his finger.

The faint outline of the web greeted Raymond through the study window. Something was in the center, not a dark shape but a light one; it couldn't be the spider, he thought. It was milky white in color and nearly as big as a man's hand.

He rummaged through the kitchen closet for a can of Raid, then found a flashlight in the garage. Cautiously, he made his way down the deck's stairs, scanning the porch for the broom, which lay a few feet from the spider's web; however, the web was now empty. Raymond crawled along the porch toward the broom, but the thought of the spider dropping down on him from above was too much, and he went back inside.

In the storeroom, he found his old fencing mask and jacket on a shelf behind a box of Christmas decorations. He donned them and went back to the kitchen. If the spider was no longer in the web, where was it? Could it have slipped in through the crack in the door? He searched the floor of the kitchen, prepared himself, and stepped outside.

On his hands and knees he made his way toward the broom, surveying the deck rafters above with the flashlight. He caught sight of a white leg moving swiftly behind the redwood plank to the right of his head. He dropped the flashlight. "Damn it!"

Grabbing the broom, he waved it over his head with one hand while searching for the flashlight with the other. It was within reach; he picked it up and panned the light behind the rafter. The web was behind him now; he turned toward it, readying the broom in his hand. The spider sat, perched at the edge of the silky strands: hairless, wet and sticky. He struck at it with the broom but was off balance, his swipe feeble. Did he hit it? He jumped back off the porch onto the grass, the broom raised over his head like a sword, the can of Raid like a shield.

The spider re-appeared from the shadows at the back of the porch, heading toward him, trying to make it to the safety of the dark grass. Raymond dropped the flashlight and stepped toward it, raising the can of repellant and spraying. The spider kept coming; he sprayed again, emptying the can. It staggered slowly. He stood in the safety of the grass two feet from the spider and watched it struggling. Only four of its legs were functioning, and they seemed to move in slow motion, yet they were still able to pull the huge bulk of the abdomen. It was in the shape of an octagon, thick, with two black dots at the tail end that Raymond hadn't noticed before. The spider neared the edge of the porch, dragging its body along the cement.

He slammed the broom down, smashing it again and again. When he finally dropped the broom, there were a few legs stuck to the pavement, and the thick abdomen had flattened out, spewing milky juice.

Strewn about the spider's remains, a cotton-like substance shimmered within the juice. He examined it, tried to sweep it away with the broom, but it seemed to smear and stick on the pavement.

In their bedroom, Carol lay peacefully under the covers. He pulled back the blankets and stared at the glow of her white body. Climbing on top of her, he felt her breast with his hand. The stiffening in his groin excited him. Kissing her, he pushed himself against her.

"Ray, what are you doing?" Carol pushed him away. "Not now!" She rolled onto her side, her back to him. "Let me sleep."

Raymond rolled away and stared out the window at the fingers of the leafless branch.

He didn't wake with his alarm the next morning, nor did he when the snooze went off five minutes later. The spider appeared in his dreams again and again. Each time he killed it, and each time the spider returned bigger and stronger. When it burst through the bedroom door, the size of a mastiff, he awoke. Carol was not in the bed.

He went downstairs. She was nowhere in sight. "Carol!" he yelled. "Carol!" The stove clock read eight. She would already be at work. Lifting the phone from the receiver, he started to dial her office, then stopped and hung up the handset. No, he said to himself, everything would be all right. He made himself a latté and walked out onto the deck. It was going to be a scorcher, the morning sun already hot. Maybe he'd surprise her. Get the place fixed up. He could get the tree service out to trim the branches that hung down over his back fence; maybe an exterminator would eliminate the bugs; and surely a call to the city's wildlife division would put an end to the screaming raccoons.

Rather than filling his empty stomach, the latté had soured it. He decided that granola and plain yogurt would help. But then he felt a tickling on his foot. A tiny white spider ran across his big toe. He kicked it away. It couldn't be, he thought. It couldn't have been eggs. With trepidation, he walked down the deck stairs to the porch.

He would call her and tell her, and then everything would be all right again. They could discuss issues, she could help him with his work, they might even get some fish, they're not too messy—one of those large aquariums would look great in the living room. He turned the corner at the bottom of the stairs.

Hundreds, if not thousands, of tiny, white spiders scuttled about the porch, a line of them already crawling up the deck post, making their way onto the upper deck and inside the house.

Something Like a Plan

We didn't think of ourselves as scientists or even engineers. But that's what we were. All those hours gluing balsa wood and plastic. The careful cutting of the outline with the X-Acto knife. The alignment of fins with fuselage. Like NASA, we started small, first launching the Mosquito and the Swift, working out telemetries and landing sites, then moving on to Big Bertha and our attempts to compensate for cargo load. We weighed our future astronauts, lizards we'd caught in the field behind our house, but it was difficult to get an accurate measurement—an ounce or two at most. We trained them for their mission and kept them off-hours in a shoe box at Bill's house. We spared no expense, furnishing their home away from home with little beds, sofas, and lawn chairs from Bill's sister's Barbie castle. We even included sand and a bathing pool. Of course, the Loadstar II was our ultimate objective. With it's advanced two-stage launch sequence, utilizing both C6 and C6-7 engines, it could reach heights of over one thousand feet. Most important, however, was the large clear plastic payload section—the perfect size for one astronaut to make a heroic journey.

We checked weather reports and marked our calendars. Time, date, and location had been meticulously set. The elementary school playground offered the best surface. It was large, and even if the wind carried the parachute astray, the payload section would most likely land on the roof, and we were veterans of scaling those walls. We chose the lizard, fitted him in his little astronaut suit of tin foil, and marched in mass to the launch site. After playing Strauss' *Also Sprach Zarathustra* on Rob's boom box, we saluted our astronaut and placed him into the cargo bay. Of course, we had enough sense to do this at the last moment. We were not idiots. We knew the air supply in the payload section would be limited. The count-down began. Bill lit the fuse, and we ran to the safety perimeter. The much safer electronic ignition system having not yet been invented.

Ten, nine, eight, seven, six . . . We have a go for main engine start. . . five, four, three, two, one . . . booster ignition and lift off. The bird is in the air. The music of Strauss soared. We cheered and hugged each other just as we'd seen mission control do after the Apollo launch. Everything had gone as planned. We watched as our spaceship rose higher and higher, until it was just a speck. Then it was gone beyond our sight. Even John, who had the sense to bring his dad's binoculars couldn't spot it. We forgot the clouds that drifted above. We forgot the rising strings of Strauss. We forgot the butterflies flitting by and the ants soldiering on around us, forgot the stories we sometimes told each other late at night, forgot that Rob's mom cried so loudly in her room after the divorce that on sleep overs we had to turn the volume of the TV all the way up, forgot that Bill had taken to holing up in his room recently, playing Pink Floyd over and over and leaving scary notes for his mom, notes his mom said forced her to register him at a "hospital" in the fall, forgot that John's dad rarely came home sober and the one night he did, they found him locked in the bathroom with a gun. He said he was only cleaning it. Forgot the sisters who'd been hospitalized for Lyme disease, the brothers who'd been in car accidents, the uncles who invited us to see their dirty magazines and the aunts who told us no matter how much we washed we would never be clean enough. We forgot everything about our puny lives. And then John spotted the parachute.

How fast is it falling? we asked. *Is it coming straight down or drifting on the breeze?* Our biggest worry had been the return. We'd done tests with rocks in the payload bay and dropped the parachute from the rooftop of Bill's two-story, but there was no way to test for a fall of a thousand feet. We held our breath and watched. It drifted right, then left, coming dangerously close to the school roof. But, somehow, as if we actually knew what we were doing, as if all our pseudo-science had paid off, the payload section came to a soft landing in the grass.

It's difficult to describe the feeling as we cautiously

approached. The clear plastic of the payload bay had been scorched black, so we couldn't see the lizard inside. "Somebody open it!" Rob shouted. "Get that lizard out before he suffocates or burns or . . ." We looked one to another unsure what to do. What if it was dead? Or worse, burned to a crisp? What if the mission was a failure? After all, what did it matter that we sent a lizard into space if it couldn't return to tell about it? "What if the ship's still hot?" John asked. "Those burn marks look bad." Bill stepped forward and scooped up the rocket. "I don't care," he said as he pried open the payload section, ready to cover it with his hand in case the lizard scrambled out. Nothing happened. "Is it alive?" Rob asked, stepping closer. Bill tilted the rocket so that the lizard slid out onto his hand. He brought his face closer, tapping it with his finger. "It's breathing," he said. "Just barely, but it's breathing."

That first day we nursed him back to health. Gave him crickets, flies, whatever he wanted. We even let him lounge about by the pool in his shoebox. We huddled around him every moment as if we couldn't get enough. Our hero. The astronaut who escaped our planet's gravitational pull and disappeared somewhere we could only guess at, some beyond that held untold mysteries, that offered visions of our world of which we could only dream. We made plans for a second mission and a third. *What if we tried the Protostar? It uses*

C, D, and E engines. I hear it can go 1500 feet! We talked about what great scientific discoveries lay ahead, our need to solve the mysteries of the universe, and what might happen once we'd done so. *We'll be rich and famous! We'll get jobs with NASA!* There was no limit to our dreaming.

The next morning, we converged on Bill's house, once again huddling around our lizard, wishing he could tell us everything he'd seen. He didn't seem to care, didn't do much at all, in fact. It was as if the whole thing meant nothing to him. We tried to feed him more crickets, but he wouldn't touch them. Even when they crawled over him, he let them. He'd seen everything, gotten everything he'd wanted, and now, he'd stopped caring. "He sucks!" Rob said, flicking sand on him. "Yeah, he totally bites," John joined in. By noon, we were selling rocks door-to-door. They weren't anything special, just rocks we'd found in the field. If we made enough, we could buy ice cream later. Maybe even a blow pop. Only Bill continued to hover over the shoebox, watching the lizard, as though whatever light lay hidden inside might yet touch him. Soon, he, too, gave up and joined us, painting some of the rocks gold so they'd fetch a better price. By evening, we'd forgotten about our space program entirely. By mid-week, all three astronauts had escaped the shoebox. We'll never know what happened to two of them, but we found the remains of one on the mouth of Bill's cat. Was it our astronaut? The one who broke free of this world? We choose to think not. We choose, rather, to believe that there's always one more equation, a plan B, a way of escaping the unseen trajectories of our carefully plotted lives.

The Silence that Follows

This morning I am born a stranger to myself. Yesterday, my life was open doors and birdsong. The sweet, sharp smell of grass. The dark fragrance of earth. Now I pass a life in plastic. I can't see, can't scent a thing except a moldy, cheesy smell, which I can only assume is the plastic. I try pawing it off but I get yelled at. And then the look. I try again when he leaves for work, but it's part of me now. Something happened in the night. Had I done something terribly wrong? I remember the sting of pain near my groin when running by the woods at the edge of the yard. I remember the tangy taste of blood when I licked the wound after. I remember being wrapped in a towel and placed in the back of the car, only not for a walk like I'd thought. And I remember the man in white approaching with something sharp in his hand. Nothing else.

Nothing makes sense now. Not that it did even before the Event. But at least there was an order to my day. I could look forward to a range of scents, even a few small surprises—fresh scat of deer or raccoon in the yard. Now only the sadness of moldy cheese. And the fact that I can no longer walk without bumping into things. It's like my head has grown three sizes larger. Scouring the floor of the kitchen for any breakfast that might have dropped, I run into the table, the chairs. Panicked, I run back to my crate. That's when I see my reflection in the sliding glass door. It's me, but where my head should be, there's a cone. I don't know how it got there. I don't know how to get it off. I don't even know if it's a part of me. How did life become so un-recognizable?

I don't even lift my gargantuan head when he returns. What's the point? He says something I don't understand. His tone is nice but it doesn't change the world I've woken into. He bounces the ball and speaks again, then throws it across the kitchen. Why bother? I can't pick it up. Doesn't he realize that? Doesn't he understand that everything's changed.

After dinner, he sits in his chair and reads. It's a big book. One he's been reading for as long as I can remember, which is admittedly not very long. He seems happy. When he goes to bed, he lays the Book on the chair. I go back to sleep, but it's impossible to get comfortable. And every time I open my eyes I see the Book. It seems bigger somehow than before. Slowly, I approach. It smells like an old room. The fact that I can smell it is not lost on me.

I paw at the Book, and it falls face down to the floor with a thud. On the back, there's a picture of a man kneeling and smiling, his arm around the dog beside him. *I don't know resurrection.* The Voice scares me because it both sounds like mine and not like mine. Maybe it's mine amplified by the cone. I step back. *Transfiguration pierces me, tears me open.* Again the Voice. I run in circles to escape it. How did it know? I go back to my crate, catching the cone on the sides when I turn to lie down. The noise is worse than the Voice. I run from my crate. And again, there is the Book.

I lie with It, and doing so brings comfort, but not peace. I need to know what It says. What It is. I paw at It. The back cover flips open, but almost as quickly closes. I paw at It again, the smell of It driving me on. The old room smell that also now seems mixed with vanilla and almonds. The smell hanging in the air like a question. *Do you believe?* Then, it's like I'm digging a hole in the back yard. I can't stop myself. Scraps of pages fly right and left, and yet I'm no closer to an answer. I push my face into what remains of the Book, the cone jamming into the floor, keeping me from touching It. I can't even lick it. Can't taste It. Can't get close enough to lap up the pages. The Voice in the back of my head says, *How do you want the Book of Hope to taste?* And I can't answer because I don't know. The fact that I don't know angers me more than the cone, and I jam my face into the book.

The front of the cone slams into the floor, pushing back against my neck, cutting into it with the force. The pain clears my head, and I tear into the Book. I tear Its pages out, tear them to shreds, and it feels good, as if destruction is the only way to move forward through the cone-shaped dream that has become my world.

When it's over, I gather the scraps like wingless birds. Some of the pieces have pictures. One of a dog running. Another getting a treat. I pile the pieces into my bed and lie on them. *You don't know resurrection,* the Voice says. The Voice I thought I'd torn out. *You can destroy me, but like the fly I will return.*

The waiting is worse than life with the cone. Worse than the Book before the book was no more. And the Voice is worse than the waiting. The Voice tells me I should recoil from everything that makes up my world. The Voice says I should piece the scraps together to understand. And so I do. I put a half torn picture of a man throwing a ball in an open field next to a torn photo of a dog eating a treat. But they don't fit right. I try another photo, this time of a puppy held in an arm. You can't see what body the arm belongs too because the page is torn. I don't know if it's a man or woman or even a child. I place the photo next to a scrap that shows half of a dog's face holding half a newspaper in its mouth. At least I think it's a newspaper. It could be a magazine. Or maybe even a treat. The photo is so scratched I can't be sure. The more I try to piece things together, the worse things become.

When he wakes and returns to the kitchen, The

Voice reminds me to recoil. And so I do. I back as far into my crate as I can, gathering the broken and torn pages of the Book beneath me. I wait in the darkness and listen. He doesn't seem to notice me, just mumbles something under his breath, as he eats. I want to go to him. I want things to be like they were before the Event. But the Voice tells me things will never be like they were. The Voice tells me I must wait in the dark until things change once again. I want to go to him and lick the butter from his hand the way I used to, but I know even if I tried, I would not able to do it. The Voice reminds me to wait. To wait in the dark. But I want to go to him, I say back to the Voice. I want to stand with him by the door until he takes me out to pee, just like he used to do. *Fool!* the Voice says. *Those days will not come again. Not until the resurrection.*

And so I wait. But the truth is I will never die. The Book told me this. Not in so many words. Not with words at all. But in the Silence that follows between the torn and wounded pictures. Such is the length of this life I no longer recognize.

In the Dream You Were Large

We became trapped in the car on our fourth date. I was sure she was the one and had planned on asking her that night to mate for life. I know what you're thinking. Bats are promiscuous. They love to fool around. And I'll admit, I've used my sperm plug in the past to make sure whoever I was hot on didn't two-time me, but this was different. We'd waited. I even asked her if I could kiss her. Then one thing led to another and soon we were having sex in the back seat. It was transcendent. I couldn't tell where I ended and she began. After, we fell asleep on the seat. That's when the humans must have arrived.

Don't rush to judgement. It was a cold October night on the north side of Chicago, and mating season was nearing an end. You can't blame us for seeking some shelter. I woke immediately and tried to shake Cecilia awake. I had no idea she'd be such a heavy sleeper. She peeled open one beautiful eye, and I pointed to the open rear window through which we'd entered. But just as I pulled her to an upright position several things happened simultaneously. In fact, it all happened so fast, and the events that followed were so traumatic, I'm not even sure of the order now or even of my part.

I'm pretty sure the rear doors opened on both sides.

There were voices. Loud voices joking and laughing. There was only a moment to act. And my action, or lack of it, is the first of many things to haunt me from that night. I'd like to think I held on to her, grabbed her with my rear claw, and pulled her into the air in an attempt to fly past the bodies entering the car. I'd like to believe a stray elbow knocked her from my grasp, that I was not able to make it back to her, and so climbed the back seat just before the humans sat because I thought I'd caught a glimpse of her climbing as well. I'd like to think that when I saw the seat-belt hook on the ceiling of the car near the open window, I climbed toward it, not to escape but to gain a better vantage from which I could sound her location. Three people sat in that back seat. The driver closed the rear window, and I was left clutching the seat-belt hook. That's what I tell myself happened anyway. I wouldn't have simply abandoned her at the first sign of trouble. I couldn't have done that.

One of the passengers reached behind her to grab the seat belt. She didn't look behind her thankfully but rather pawed at the belt, grazing me with her fingers as she did so. "What a funny feeling seatbelt!" she exclaimed. "It's like big fuzzy dice." I held on tight with my rear claws and prayed she wouldn't turn around. After a few more paws, she found the belt and cinched it about her. That's when I heard Cecilia's muffled cries, as if she were calling me from deep underground. Those cries still haunt me. I hear them even now as I tell this tale for the thousandth time.

In my dreams I imagine myself hanging upside down, spreading my wings wide, and hissing wildly until the passengers turned around and fled in horror from the car. Sometimes I even see myself crawling across the car ceiling, then hanging there before their eyes, spreading my wings in all their glory. Then I rescue Cecilia from the seat where she's been trapped, pinned beneath the hindquarters of one of them. In my dreams, she's still okay. A little worse for the wear, but she's able to fly out the door the passengers left open when they ran screaming from the car.

The truth is, I hid, hanging upside down in the back from that seat belt hook, my wings folded around me, trying to block out Cecilia's cries, sounds outside the hearing range of humans, but unfortunately, not mine. Time flipped backwards and forwards, up and down, so that I have no idea how long we were in that car. Five minutes. Half an hour. An hour. Time, like so much of my life that night, lost all meaning. We stopped, and for a moment, as the passengers stepped out of the car, I had hope.

But then I saw her, sputtering and flapping on the seat, spinning in wounded circles. She let out another cry, this time in a lower frequency. "No!" I yelled. "Please, no! I'll get you out of here, but you've got to be quiet!" In her pain, she didn't or couldn't hear me. She cried out again, fluttering there in the middle of the seat. And that's when one of the passengers heard her cries. A woman. She turned around and screamed, pointing at Cecilia. "Oh my God!," she yelled. "I sat on a bat!" The others laughed at first, thinking she was joking. But then they heard Cecilia, too, and saw her flapping about the seat. "Jesus! Amy sat on a god-damned bat!" they said. In the confusion, I knew I had a brief moment in which to act. But no matter how hard I willed myself I didn't move. "Fly away, Cecilia!" I shouted." "Hurry, please! While you have time!"

The one they called Amy grabbed a stick and knocked Cecilia from the seat. She landed on the pavement next to the car, where she continued her writhing. "What'll we do?" one of the humans asked. "We should put it out of its misery," Amy replied. "Good idea," the others agreed. The driver pulled his keys from his pocket and reached for the front door. "Stop!" I yelled and flew out into the night, shrieking at the lowest frequency I could muster and flying as close to their faces as I could. At least that's the way I choose to remember it. They screamed and swatted at me, but I was too quick for them. I darted in and out, dive bombing them over and over until the driver said. "Listen guys, do you see that line. The haunted house is going to close soon, and we might not make it if we don't hurry. I vote we leave the bat. It'll be dead by the time we return." Though Amy hesitated, the rest murmured their assent, and, in the end, she went to stand in line with them. I was left alone with Cecilia.

Did I go to her? I'd like to believe I did. I'd like to think she died in my wings, as I held her close to me and sang our song. *O, my love. My darling. I hunger for your touch.* That's the way I remember it happening. It's what I tell myself happened. Whether I held her or not, I remember flying over that long line that led into the haunted house. I remember swooping down and grabbing at women's hair, clawing at men's faces, doing everything I could to scare them, to make them feel a fraction of the pain they'd caused me. And I remember, too, the vision of the haunted house rising before me. I remember how I caught sight of the shadow of a bat with red lights for eyes, bobbing up and down on a string in the second story window, as if mocking me. I remember thinking as I soared off into the light of the full moon, how nice to be like that bat, to have no memory of our part in this absurd world.

We were swimming along in the lake, minding our own business, Catherine and I, when we came across a murder of boys standing in the shallows arguing over who got to hold the two bows they'd brought along with them. Four boys, two bows. It shouldn't have been much of a problem. They could have taken turns. But they didn't think of that. In the end, the boy with the baseball hat on backwards grabbed one of the bows out of the hands of the boy who had on a shirt that read "Make Tea, Not War," and the boy with the buzz cut tripped the boy with the droopy face, then grabbed the other bow. I told Catherine maybe it would be best if we high tailed it out of the shallows, but she'd never encountered boys before, never seen animals splash around so much, make so much noise. A constellation of joy and danger. She wanted to move in closer. I tried to stop her, but she's never listened to me anyway.

"This is so rad, Peter," the boy with the buzz cut said. "I can't believe you have your own pond on your property."

Peter must have been the boy with the t-shirt because he smiled, then bent to pick up a pebble to hide his pride.

"Yeah, if I lived here," the boy with the baseball hat said. "I'd be outside every day."

"I come out here a lot," Peter replied. "Walking the woods, or just hanging by the pond listening to the frogs."

"What do the frogs say?," buzz cut said, punching Peter in the shoulder.

"Thanks, Floyd," Peter replied. "I needed that."

"I get it," the boy with the droopy face joined in. "It's nice here."

"Shut up, Rob!" baseball hat said.

"You shut up, Lance!" Rob shot back.

"Seriously, we should camp tonight." Peter stepped between them. "Let's have a sleep over. We'll pitch a tent right here by the pond." He kicked away rocks and branches to clear an area.

"Awesome," the boys agreed, nodding their heads, puffing up just a little as they took in the pine-scented air. For a brief moment, all their frenzied movement stopped.

A few stray clouds floated overhead in the Colorado sky. The cottonwoods scattered about the pines whispered to each other in the mid-afternoon breeze. The prairie grass and goldenrod around the pond murmured in their own tongues. It was a moment where anything could have happened, when things could go one way or the other. Anyone could feel it. An act of tenderness or cruelty could lead to a shift in the fabric of the world.

"Hey, what's that?" Rob pointed to the water. He walked further into the pond.

"I think it's a fish," Peter said, joining him. "And a big one, too."

They pointed at Catherine, who was treading water peacefully in the shallows not ten feet from where they stood. She looked so calm, opening her mouth like she wanted to communicate with them.

"It's beautiful, the way it shimmers like that," Floyd added, the bow in his hand. "Like it has a rainbow painted on its side."

"Yeah," Rob said. "I think it's because they have oily skin. I read that somewhere."

I don't know what it was about that moment that scared me so. The boys' faces showed no hint of meanness. If anything, they were curious, even vulnerable the way they stared, eyes as open as morning. Then the jaybird released his terrible, monotonous cry. I didn't think. I darted to Catherine. The boys jumped back. I could see Lance raise his bow from the shoreline, shooting past the boys, the arrow flying just an inch over Floyd's shoulder, before impaling the mud barely a foot from Catherine.

"What the fuck, man?" Floyd yelled. "You trying to kill me."

In answer, Lance ran into the shallows while notching another arrow. As if caught in Lance's tide, Floyd, too, notched an arrow, both letting loose at the same time. Two arrows stabbed the mud on either side of me.

"What's happening?" Catherine asked.

"We've got to get out of here now!" I shouted, then turned to lead the way.

Arrows hissed by, one after the other, in the water. A few more feet, and we'd be free of the shallows. I turned back to make sure Catherine was right behind me. It was then, an arrow impaled her side, pinning her to the mud.

The boys surrounded her immediately, standing in the knee-deep water, excitement limning their faces. "Nice shot, Floyd," Lance said. "Yeah, that was amazing," Rob said. "All those arrows. It was like a thousand birds flying past us."

There was nothing I could do as they dragged Catherine to shore, her mouth opening and closing.

"Why's it doing that?" Rob asked.

"I think it's trying to breathe," Peter replied.

"They breathe through gills, man. Not their mouths," Lance said, shaking his head.

The boys stared at her unsure what to do. The breeze stilled. The goldenrods hushed.

"How long til it dies?" Floyd asked.

"Maybe we should shoot it again," Rob said. "I mean, help it to die."

They shot an arrow straight through her side, and still her mouth opened and closed, opened and closed. They shot again and again.

"Why won't it die!" Peter cried. "What's the matter with it!"

Whatever excitement the boys had felt before was gone, replaced by the horror of watching Catherine speaking to them from another world. The sun beat down. The jaybird cried again. And still her mouth opened and closed.

"Somebody stop it!" Rob shouted, turning away and walking a few feet up the shore before slumping in the dirt.

Without a word, Lance picked up a large rock and bashed in Catherine's head. Her mouth only moved more frantically. Lance brought the rock down again and again until all that was left was a bloody pulp. He threw the rock in the water, "What the fuck was wrong with that fish?" he said, then threw his bow and arrows on the ground beside Rob and sat down. Peter and Floyd staggered over to join them.

I couldn't leave. I couldn't stay. I didn't know what to do, where to go. I wanted to die but could not. It was as if everything that had happened was replaying in me, would continue to replay in me over and over again. My life would never be the same. And that's when I saw the boys lying on the sand, like corpses marooned under a desert sun. They stared at the scattered clouds as if demanding another kind of seeing, one that would allow for the face they wanted, one that wouldn't vacillate between touching the immeasurable heart of the world and killing everything in it.

I was also told to stop making holes. Of course, I had to eat. My therapist acknowledged that. But you don't need to make holes to eat, at least not big ones. A little pecking here, a little hammering there, and you can find all the larvae and bugs you want. It was my need to make the holes deep, to make vast caverns within the trees that was the problem. She said those hollow trees were a reflection of my own emptiness. What do you say back to that? Nothing. Or at least that's what I said. A big fat nothing. That's why I'm hammering away at cedar shingles now. I've already drilled several good holes, nests any family would want to live in. The problem is I lost my family.

I should have seen it coming, should have known from the thousand little fights, and worse should have seen the signs once we stopped fighting, once we stopped caring enough to fight. "Hon, I'm going to the meadow with some friends. You can do whatever you want today," my wife said on so many Sundays. Or, "Hon, I'll be in the birch grove today, everyone's getting together to throw the neighbors a baby shower. You have fun by yourself." In the end, she said I spent too much time "working," by which she meant I spent too much time digging holes.

So, I sit on the side of this house, drilling here, drilling there. Last week, I found the perfect spot. Tender wood. Grub filled. With potential for expansion. And there's a window to the right of it, where I can take a break from the head pounding and look into another world, while still maintaining my foothold on the shingles. The window opens to a family room with a couch, two reclining chairs, a fireplace, and a TV set. There's a man sitting in one of the recliners facing the window. He's been there nearly every day. He doesn't seem to do much except sit there staring at the computer screen on his laptop and occasionally typing. Once in a while he picks up the cell on the armrest and looks at that, too. Maybe he's working. I don't know. Sometimes, a dog enters the room from the adjoining kitchen and puts his big ugly brown head on the armrest of the chair. The man sometimes absentmindedly pets the dog, but when he does, it only lasts a minute or two. Then the dog gives up and leaves. Sometimes, the dog spots me in the window and barks. I hate dogs. The man doesn't even look at the window when the dog barks.

And then it happens. On the seventh morning, a little boy walks into the room and stands before the man. I didn't even know the man had a son. I'd certainly seen no evidence of it before. The boy asks a question. Of course, I can't hear it, but his lips are moving, so that's what I assume he's doing. The man doesn't hear it at first either. He keeps typing on his little laptop. The boy repeats himself. The man still doesn't hear. The boy's shoulders sag. He's clearly dejected. I've seen that look a thousand times before. He steps back and starts to walk away. "Hey!" I shout, hammering on the glass. *Tap. Ta—Tap, Tap!* "Hey! What are you doing? Your boy's trying to talk to you!" The man doesn't look up, but the boy squeals with delight, says something and points in my direction. He turns back to the man, speaking to him. The man raises his head, smiles and says, "That's nice." I can read his lips only because they mirror what I've said to my own children so many times before. He returns his attention to his laptop. The boy approaches the glass, looks at me for a long moment, then runs off. I crane my neck to follow him as long as I can and manage to see him skipping around the kitchen before he vanishes. As quickly as my own kids, he's gone. Just like that.

The forest behind winks. The sun spins around me in a wobbly orbit. I no longer recognize my own re-flection in the window, the red crest and long, pointed beak belong to someone else. I cry out but my voice is no longer my own. "Hey!" the voice shouts, ham-mering on the window. *Tap, Ta—Tap, Tap!* "What's the matter with you?" The man pays no attention, so I hammer harder. "Hey! Look at yourself! What do you think you're doing?" *Ta-Tap, Ta-Tap, Ta-Tap, Tap, Tap,*

Tap! Still, he keeps typing on his precious computer. The weight of the forest presses down on me until I see only darkness. I hammer at the window harder and harder until I break through in a shimmering of shattered glass. It's only then that the man stops what he's doing and looks up. "What the . . .?" he starts to say. But I'm on him, my claws firmly fixing on his nose, my beak drilling over and over into his forehead. *Tap, Ta-Tap, Tap, Ta-Tap, Tap.* The man screams, tries to fight me off. But it's too late. I've broken through the hard bark to the precious grub beneath. I don't even know what I'm saying. It doesn't matter. My words are small, poor. Like the grub I eat. I know only that I must keep hammering, hollowing him out to make another nest. If only I can make this one bigger. Better. A place where my own emptiness won't stare back.

They're Not That Big

If you're going to stare at a human naked in his bedroom, you should be naked, too. That's what my mother always said. And there he is, lying in bed, clutching some object, a small bell, I think. And here I am, shivering beneath an empty sky. She also said, a little bit of hammering goes a long way. So that's what I do. One quick smack against the window with my forepaws then ducking beneath the sill so all he sees is the dark staring back. The Native Americans didn't call us tricksters for nothing. The Powhatan called us *aroughcun*, which roughly translated means, "He who rubs, scrubs, and scratches with his hands." Well, these hands are good for a lot more than scratching.

I can almost feel him, his face so close his breath fogs the glass, his eyes as inscrutable as the hydrangea on the northeast corner of the house. *Would he laugh if he discovered me or try to hurt me?* Humans are the leading cause of death for our kind. No joke. But then again, where's the thrill if you play it safe? They don't call us party animals for nothing. His fingers press against the pane, as if his sense of touch were as strong as ours, as if he could somehow divine the night. I wait a moment. Two. Three. Four. Then jump up, both paws hitting the glass. If eyes could speak, his would say, "What the f….?" I didn't know humans could run so fast. I think he's hiding in the closet until he emerges, holding a small sun in his hand. I scurry to the hydrangea and watch as he flashes that thing back and forth across the grass. When he gives up, I move back to the window to see what more trouble I can cause.

He's in bed again, holding that bell. I think about jumping up, maybe scratching on the glass this time, but something about the way he's holding the bell stops me. He's clutching it as if it's everything he ever had. I raise a forepaw to the glass, and for a moment I'm inside the room with him—or at least that's how it feels. I don't know how to explain it. It just happens. Like each of his breaths is a nest of thorns on my head. The weight of the night on his chest is almost too much, and all I can think about is how I wish I could lift him up and carry him home. But then I wonder if this *is* his home, and maybe he needs to be delivered from it. They say we're smart, maybe smarter than the fox. But try as I might, I can't figure this one out. I wait there, touching that window most of the night, the empty sky pouring by. They say our hands are second only to humans. And that hands are good at almost everything. They can strum a guitar or crack open a crayfish. It's a myth that we use our hands to wash our food. The truth is we use them to see. All that scrubbing and rubbing is just a way for us to know what we have, to know if it's enough.

Sumptuous Are the Colors of the World

The boy climbs the apple tree with a hunger, grabbing branch after branch, searching foothold after foothold, as the sun burns away the thick sea of morning mist. He wants more than anything to frame his own little picture of the world from atop the tree, to see his own perfect kingdom of sky in its thousand diaphanous layers. He climbs with faith, not looking where he places his hands. So at first he doesn't feel the hairy skin of the caterpillar. He doesn't notice its plump, finger-thick body until he's grabbed the branch above his head and pulled himself half-way up. He jerks his hand back and nearly falls. Green goo sticks to his fingers. He wretches, wipes his hand on the trunk without thinking, then pulls himself up to look at the remains. Tiny red, orange, and yellow hairs dot the pulpy, green mess. What he thinks must be the head is still intact, rising out of the slime, not flattened like the rest. It nods slowly back and forth, as if denying the reality of what's happened. The boy wretches again. But he can't turn away. He watches for what must be a half hour until the head finally stops moving. Then he climbs down and wanders the neighborhood into early afternoon, paying no attention to the requiem of dandelion fluff floating around him, the light of the sun trembling on the green leaves, or the footprint of birds on the clear blue sky.

This could be a story about love, about how easy it is to forget. It could be a story about home, what it means to feel safe. Or it could be about the lessons we learn, how they're not always what we might think. *Just because you can't see them doesn't mean they're not there.* What we do know is that the boy never climbed another tree. If we could chart his life, we would see how quickly the days began running past. First one, then another, and another, until he lived in a world so far outside of things there was nothing left to get in the way.

The Secret

Stan had been keeping a secret from those around him for a very long time. A big secret. He kept the secret from his wife. He kept the secret from his parents who had since passed on. He kept the secret from his two children who had moved out of the house. And he kept the secret from his brother and sister, with whom he rarely spoke.

A year ago the secret had been the size of a golf ball, or more accurately, a baby mouse. He wouldn't have discovered it at all if he hadn't started seeing a masseuse to deal with the neck and upper back pain he'd been having. "You might want to have that lump looked at," his masseuse had said. "It moves a bit when I touch it, almost like it's alive." Of course, he never did anything about it, the same way he never did anything about his dream of traveling now that his kids had grown, the same way he failed to face his quickly approaching retirement. His own parents had retired early then wasted away with nothing to do, until each had forgotten who they were, who the other was, until they'd forgotten everything about their puny lives.

The secret kept growing. He often woke complaining of a stiff neck or soreness behind the shoulder blade. But his wife was used to his complaints, so she ignored him. And at sixty-four, he was used to aches and pains, so he ignored them as well. Life could have continued on like this until long into their retirement when they spent their days sitting in opposite rooms, he watching nonstop cable news and obsessing over the state of the Republican party, and she crocheting blankets in a little craft room she'd set up for herself in the basement, blankets piled high along every wall. He could have lived on that way until he passed quietly from this world, his children saying a few words at the funeral, then slipping back into their normal routines until, after a few years, he was gone from even their memories. Yes, he could have done this. But the secret could not.

By this point, it was as large as a baseball, and it had started to move. Not much at first, mostly it restricted itself to his neck and upper back. But over time, its territory grew. At first, Stan was a bit surprised by the occasional shifting of the lump in his back. But then he found it oddly pleasing. He would absentmindedly prod it while eating breakfast or reading the paper, poking it to see if he could get it to move. When it would, he'd experience a small thrill as little claws scurried across his back. He'd then return to his routine only to find himself poking the lump again a few minutes later and waiting for the tickle of little feet. For the most part, it didn't move much during the day, and for the most part, Stan didn't worry about it.

The problem came at night. He'd always been a back sleeper, and now he couldn't do it. In the king-sized bed he and his wife shared, he could shift and flail about trying to get comfortable and not bother her in the slightest. He'd never been good at sleeping on his side, but now it was near impossible. As soon as he fell asleep on his left side, he'd feel those little feet scamper to that very side as if the secret sought the warmth between his back and the bed. Like a cat kneading a pillow, it would dig its claws into the muscle below his shoulder blade (its favorite spot) or the trapezius (its second favorite spot), and he would have to switch sides to get a few minutes of peace before it would decide it wanted to switch sides, too. Then there were the times it had the "night crazies" and would scurry about his back in circles and zigzags so that he had no hope for even a few minutes of rest.

Still, Stan was resilient, better than most at ignoring the aches and pains and lack of sleep that constituted the body's only form of communication with the man. Despite the growing pain in his upper back he went about his days much as he had before. Certainly, he used a little more Advil than the average man. He was a bit sleepier than usual, but closing his office door and taking a mid-afternoon catnap usually solved that problem.

It was only when he realized the secret was eating

him from the inside, had been eating him all along, that things began to change. At first, he tried to compensate by increasing his caloric intake, but that could only work for so long. Soon the pain of shredded muscle and torn sinew became difficult to ignore. No amount of Advil could hide it.

The first thing he tried was talking to his wife. "Something is happening in my back," he told her late one night. "I think I might be dying." She was already in bed, when he slipped in beside her. She lowered her book and asked what kind of insurance he had.

"I'm not worried about whether it will be covered," he said.

"Not that kind of insurance." She folded her arms over her chest the way a funeral director might prepare a corpse. "Life insurance. How much do you have?" Her gaze remained fixed on the ceiling as if somehow she could see through it to the pattern of stars beyond.

"I said I'm afraid I'm dying, not that I'm going to die." He pulled the covers to his chin as if to protect himself.

"What's the difference?" She turned her head to face him, but not her body.

"There's all the difference in the world!" He rolled away from her. "Do me a favor," he said, "And take a look at my back." He pulled up his nightshirt.

She groaned, then reluctantly inspected his back.

"You've got a lump just under your right shoulder blade," she said. "It looks pretty big." She touched it, and as she did, the lump moved down his spine, resting in his lower back.

"Did you see that?" he asked.

"Yes. It looks like you've got something in there." She picked up her book and continued reading.

"That's it!" he said. "That's all you're going to say." He pulled down his nightshirt and sat up, facing her. When she didn't seem to notice, he pulled the book from her hands and tossed it across the bed.

"Hey!" She shot him a look. "What did you do that for?"

Pain tore through the muscle along his upper spine. Like teeth ripping.

"Ow! Shit!" was all he managed to say. He jumped out of bed and turned on the light. Again, he pulled up his shirt. "It bit me! Hard! Can you see anything?"

"What do you want me to say?" She ran her finger along the lump. "It's a lump. I don't think a lump can bite you, but I'm not a doctor."

He went to the bathroom and tried in vain to get a good view of the lump on his back in the mirror.

"You know what they say," his wife went on. "These things are the body's way of trying to tell you something. You should have it checked out. And while you're at it, raise whatever you have for life insurance." She returned to her book, and he returned to bed. Silence settled over them.

It wasn't until the lump was eight or nine inches across and three or four thick that he decided to see a doctor. It hadn't been an easy decision for him as it meant taking the afternoon off work, and he'd had loads of work to finish since announcing his retirement. Taking the afternoon off work meant he would have time to himself, something he still hadn't grown accustomed to since his daughter had left the house the year before. The idea of sitting in his favorite chair, maybe lighting a fire, picking out one of the many books on his shelves he'd never found time to read should have been appealing to him, but it filled him with dread.

"You've got a rat in your back." The doctor didn't even bother to line the X-rays up along the lighted panels so he could see. Instead, he handed him the manila envelope containing the X-rays as if they were secret documents.

"Can you get it out?" He scratched his neck below the beard he'd started to grow.

"There's really no point." The doctor wrote something down on his prescription pad. "I don't see any long term consequences."

"But it's eating me from the inside out?" The room seemed to grow dim, as if one of the fluorescents had burnt out.

"The internal damage appears to be minimal." The doctor handed him the prescription. "Eat well balanced meals, exercise, and take one of these each day and that should compensate for any muscle loss."

"What about disease? You know, the Bubonic Plague and all that?" He couldn't help scratching again and wondered if rats carried mange, too.

"You've got more of a chance of being hit by a car than dying from the Black Death." The doctor laughed as if he'd made a joke, then held out his hand.

A trail of rat droppings, Stan thought. Little pieces of what I've been.

He didn't want to go home. The idea of being there alone was too much. He thought about stopping at the mall, but it was early December and the parking lots would be full to the brim with holiday shoppers. He could stop at Stella's, his favorite coffee shop. Yes, that would do the trick. He took a slight detour and minutes later he'd arrived. But the storefront looked empty, dark. A sign posted on the door announced the arrival of a new cell phone store. It couldn't be. He'd just been to Stella's the week before. He got out of his car and peered in the window. Bare wires stuck out of the wall where the espresso machine used to be. Scraps of dry wall lay scattered about the floor. Now there was nothing for it but to go home.

Even so, we are here.

He whipped around, instinctively sticking his hand out before him as if to ward off the source of the voice. But nothing was there. He was sure he'd heard it, a deep voice, an old man's gruff voice.

"Here where?" he replied, as if speaking to someone. "The coffee shop? It's not here any more." He had to laugh. One less thing to do in his retirement.

He couldn't remember when entering his house had become difficult. At least entering it alone. The silence. The emptiness. The way the pillows tilted on the couch. The way the kitchen chairs seemed pushed out at odd angles. The way his wife's sweater lay cast aside on the end table. All of it accusing. All of it demanding something of him, something he'd buried deep long ago. Then there was the tick, tick, ticking of the clocks in every room. There was no escaping the clocks. The reminder that he'd had his chance.

Once home, he picked the first book he spotted on the bookshelf. The title didn't matter, most of the books he'd never bothered to read, and even if it was one he'd read, he'd most certainly forgotten he'd read it by now. He lit a fire, made himself a coffee, and sat in his favorite chair, pleased with himself for facing his fear, confident in the fact that he could hide from the silence, shelter himself from the accusation of pillows and sweaters and chairs behind the cover of a good book. But scarcely had he opened his book when he thought he heard the voice again. The same one he'd heard in front of Stella's.

He closed the book. Short breaths like unfortunate stutters. The thing scurried across his back. It couldn't really be a rat. The doctor had to be wrong. He'd find a new doctor. What kind of a quack told you that you had a rat in your back then told you not to worry about it? He put the book down and waited. Intent. Daring the silence. The second hand on the mantle clock ticked.

Details darken a life until we forget the depths of our mistakes.

The voice again. He walked quickly to the bathroom, stopped in front of the vanity mirror, almost afraid to turn on the light. Some other skull crept out from behind his skin. Some other creature stared back at him, vague-eyed, from empty sockets. He turned on the light and caught sight of a rat scurrying across the floor behind him. A big one. A filthy one with matted hair and a long black tail. He grabbed the porcelain toothbrush holder and turned, holding it aloft as if to strike. But the rat wasn't there. It had been heading in the direction of the tub. There was no way it could have escaped.

He turned back to the mirror, and there it was. The rat raised on its hind legs, scratching desperately at the other side of the mirror. He smashed the toothbrush holder down against the reflection of the rat. The mirror cracked. The rat stopped for a moment, then started scratching again. He brought the toothbrush holder down hard again on top of where the rat's head should be. This time the porcelain shattered in his hand, cutting the tender flesh of his palm. Either in fear of its life or incensed by the sight of blood, the rat clawed furiously at the mirror. He went to his garage in search of something heavier, bringing back a large crescent wrench from his unused toolbox. But when he returned to the bathroom, the rat was gone.

He was seeing things. That was it. He needed to talk to someone. To calm down. His wife would be at work until after five, and she always hated it when he called her there. He could call his son, though he'd probably be sleeping the day away. And that would start them on the same old argument. What are you doing with your life? Why don't you have a job? No point in going there. He should call his daughter. He knew he should call her. He'd barely talked to her since she'd left the house the year before. Why wouldn't he call her? He didn't have an answer. How long had it been since he'd talked with her? Three months? They'd always been close. He thought they'd always been close. But then why hadn't he called her? And when she called, why did he let his wife answer? If she asked to talk with him, he always had some excuse, something that needed to be done around the house. Had something come between them? He didn't think so. But then why wouldn't he talk with her?

She picked up before the phone even rang on his end.

"How did you know I was calling?" he couldn't help but feel a pang at hearing her voice. The knowledge that she would be mad at him, maybe feel betrayed that he'd made so little effort. Better that than face the silence. Better that than wait for the claws to tear into his flesh again.

"I didn't," she replied. "I was about to call Brad, and when I picked up you were there."

"Your boyfriend?"

"Yes, Dad."

"So, you're not married yet?"

"No." She laughed a bit. He hoped she'd do that, hoped he could diffuse some of the anger. "You've been a stranger," she continued. "Everything okay?"

He opened his mouth to speak, to say something, though he wasn't sure exactly what, when a sharp pain clawed through him.

"Ow!" He nearly dropped the phone.

"Dad, what's going on?"

"Nothing." He could barely squeeze the word out. "Just a little chest pain." It felt like the rat was rummaging around inside his heart, his lungs. He was having trouble catching his breath.

"You're scaring me," she replied. "Is Mom there? Is anyone there with you?"

He didn't want this to happen. Their first conversation in so long, and now she was frightened. He'd wanted to tell her. Needed to. Yes! That's why he'd called. He was going to tell her the secret. It was time she knew the truth. Time she understood who he was. He'd tell her, then everything would be better between them.

"Alicia . . ." He wasn't at all sure what he'd say, only that he had to say it. "Alicia, . . . " His throat went gravelly, as if he would lose his voice.

"Dad? You don't sound well."

"I have something I need to tell you," he began again, choking back the phlegm. "You were only a child at the time . . . "

"Dad? What are you talking about?"

"Alicia . . . I don't expect you to understand . . ." He tried to continue, but the words were buried deep.

"What is it, Dad? What do you want to say?"

"I have to tell you something . . . " he started again, digging deeper than he'd ever gone before. Through layers and layers of rock. Past all the walls he'd erected. The vaults he'd locked tight. He was almost there. Only one door lay between him and the secret. He put his hand on the knob and hesitated. What was he waiting for?

"Dad?" his daughter broke in. "You're not making sense."

He almost shouted "Shut up!" but managed to stifle it, instead shushing his daughter.

"Dad! What the hell . . ."

He willed himself back at the door, his hand once again on the knob. "Open it!" he told himself, then, already sensing the weakness, tried again. "Open it." But the lack of resolve tugged at the words, pulling them deeper into the vault even as he spoke. He couldn't, no wouldn't do it. His knees buckled, and he whimpered like a kicked dog.

"I'm calling Mom," his daughter said. "Just stay there, and I'll call you back."

"No, don't hang up, sweetie!" But it was too late. She was gone. He set the phone down as something moved through him, a dark scuttling as if through trash. He ran to the large, round dining room mirror. One of the last things his mother had given him before she died. He lifted his shirt and cocked his head around to see if he could locate the rat. How could he not? It was as big as a football, maybe bigger. He looked like Quasimodo. He tried to hit it but couldn't reach much beyond his shoulder and only ended up hitting himself. The rat seemed to be content now in the middle of his back, tearing little bits of muscle and patting them into something, some shape. What was it making? The answer frightened him more than the secret. He knew only that he wouldn't wait around to find out.

He hadn't realized how easy it would be to buy large quantities of rat poison. He could mix a heavy dose of the small green pellets with bourbon and be rid of the rat before his wife arrived home from work. He wouldn't take enough to kill himself, just enough to kill the rat before it made whatever it was making. And the bourbon, well, that was to ease the pain. Rat poison couldn't be pleasant. He'd thought of everything. But mostly he'd thought of the fact that he'd been carrying this thing inside him for far too long and now it had affected his relationship with his wife, his children. His daughter, for God's sake! When had the secret come between them? He needed the thing out now. He needed to be done with it. One way or another.

He poured a whole box of D-con into the bourbon and sat in his favorite chair to sip it. Not bad. He couldn't taste the poison at all, so figured what the hell and downed the entire glass. Then he waited, just as he'd done earlier that morning. He looked at the same pillows, but their tilt no longer seemed to bother him. Same with the angle of the chairs and his wife's sweater. Perhaps the poison would work after all. But then there was the incessant ticking of the mantel clock. He took it outside and threw it in the trashcan. On his way in, he stumbled, nearly losing his balance. Something was not quite right with his head. The air around him went wavy. Carefully, he felt his way along the wall toward his chair.

A tormented sorrow burrowed along his spine. He doubled over. So much for the bourbon numbing the pain. The madness of claws ripping flesh. Fanged teeth gnawing their way out. He fell to his knees. It had to be its death throes. It would be over soon. All he had to do was wait it out. Then the phone rang. His daughter calling again to check on him, he was sure of it. But he couldn't answer. Not yet. There was no mouth that could utter the pain. He rose and staggered toward the dining room mirror, spinning at the last moment and slamming his back into it again and again. He stood before the fractured surface and waited to feel. Nothing. Maybe this was it, he thought. Maybe he'd killed the thing this time. The phone continued to ring. The ghost of a trickle along his spine, the moth-flutter touch of a child. It could be blood. He could have cut himself on one of the shards hanging from the wood frame. He reached behind his back, felt the football size lump. It wasn't moving. A good sign. He pulled his hand away. No blood. But then it was as if he could no longer see his hand, as if the contour of it had washed away, or as if a spot clouded his vision. He rubbed his hand against his cheek. Yes, it was still there, part of him.

Filthy knives tore at his flesh, the determined claws of his executioner. The pain dizzied. He torqued his right arm around in a desperate attempt to grab it and fling it from his body, but no matter how hard he tried, it always seemed out of reach. The rat was eating its way out of him, he was sure of it. He spun around, trying to grab it with both hands, and caught fragments of his reflection in the shards hanging from the mirror. A sliver of his receding hairline. A patch of ear, dark hair grazing the top. A slice of stubble along his neckline. The sketch of him no longer connecting.

He woke slumped against the wall beneath the broken mirror. Opposite him, in one of the dining room chairs, sat a black rat, much larger than him. His first reaction was to check his chest, his stomach, his back to see the hole where the rat must have eaten its way out. But he found nothing. The lump in his back was no longer there, either. He wondered if he were dead. He didn't think so, but he couldn't be sure. He listened for his breathing. Felt his pulse. If he was dead, his body was doing a pretty good job of keeping the news from him.

The black eyes of the rat stared back at him. Hard eyes. Terrible eyes. Eyes that fixed him in place. Pus dripped from one, as if it suffered from some sort of conjunctivitis. Chipped and yellowed fangs jutted from the corners of its mouth. Tangled and matted hair stuck out from the side of its back. Its breathing was erratic, and its right foot shook randomly.

"You don't look too good," he said.

The rat stared back with violent indifference. "Why don't you tell me?" the rat whispered. "Tell me your goddamned secret."

"You don't fool me for a second," he replied.

"There's a certain pleasure in hearing it from your lips," the rat said, its eyes like an unrelenting dimming, boring their way to the unnamed.

"No." he said, quietly at first. Then again, "No!"

Its breath stuttered. Its right foot trembled.

"I'm tired of this," he said.

The rat tapped its claw on the arm of the chair, as if to some unheard rhythm.

"Did you hear me?" he said. "I'm tired of living like this." He crawled toward the rat. It sat there, watching, waiting, as if it knew before he knew what he was about to do. When he'd crossed to the rat, its tail wrapped around his ankle. An embrace? A warning? He was surprised at how scaly it seemed. Like a snake. He stood. Up close, its eyes seemed sad. Many of its whiskers bent and broken.

He'd expected some resistance when he pulled the rat's jaws apart, and finding none, nearly ripped the corners of its mouth. Still it said nothing, not even when he reached into its throat, searching for leverage, for something to hold onto. He pulled himself inside, slithering through blood, sliding deep into the dark recesses of the rat's belly where he immediately began rummaging around, tearing away bits of muscle, pieces of sinew, and flecks of bone to make a nest for himself, or perhaps a wall, anything that might provide shelter from the uneasy knowledge that lay in wait.

ACKNOWLEDGMENTS

After the Pause "The Untelling"
Café Irreal "Learning Outcomes" and "That Which Doesn't Kill Us"
Construction "Rumination"
Ekphrastic Writing "The Harder Choice"
Filling Station "Something Like a Plan"
Flights "The Opposite of Words is Space"
Gris-Gris "They're Not That Big," "Sumptuous are the Colors of the World," and "A Violent Storm"
Juked "Everything Falls Silent"
The Kenyon Review Online "The Secret"
Necessary Fiction "Because We Too Must Run"
Pacifica Literary Review "Words Were Made for Ministration"
Phantom Drift "In the Dream You Were Large"
Popshot "How Ordinary the Revelation"
Posit "The Hole"
Thin Air Magazine "That Hole is Everything"
Word Riot "The Persistence of Spiders"

*Note: *The Body's First Lesson* was inspired by the 60's British Science Fiction film *Quatermass and the Pit* (Screened in the U.S. as *Five Million Years to Earth*)

PETER GRANDBOIS is the author of thirteen previous books. His plays have been performed in St. Louis, Columbus, Los Angeles, and New York. He is poetry editor at Boulevard and teaches at Denison University in Ohio. You can find him at

www.petergrandbois.com

www.ingramcontent.com/pod-product-compliance
Lightning Source LLC
Chambersburg PA
CBHW010347220726
48290CB00016B/2667